"Feeling better? movement of hi ps.

Heat flowed like lava to her fingertips and toes and back, swirling through her until it settled in her core. She bit her cheek to keep from moaning with pleasure.

"I feel wonderful," she answered breathlessly.

He lifted his head slightly. When she raised her gaze, she saw his firm, wide mouth soften. Was he about to kiss her? Really kiss her? Right here in the middle of running from people who were trying to kill them?

She should say something. Should stop this. Because all they were doing was seeking comfort in a dangerous situation.

The men who wanted to kill her were dangerous, but so was Harte. And right now, she wasn't sure who frightened her most.

MALLORY KANE

STAR WITNESS

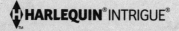
HARLEQUIN® INTRIGUE®

To Michael, for always.

Recycling programs
for this product may
not exist in your area.

ISBN-13: 978-0-373-69683-3

STAR WITNESS

Copyright © 2013 by Rickey R. Mallory

HARLEQUIN®

TM www.Harlequin.com

Printed in U.S.A.

ABOUT THE AUTHOR

Mallory has two very good reasons for loving reading and writing. Her mother was a librarian, who taught her to love and respect books as a precious resource. Her father could hold listeners spellbound for hours with his stories. He was always her biggest fan.

She loves romantic suspense with dangerous heroes and dauntless heroines, and enjoys tossing in a bit of her medical knowledge for an extra dose of intrigue. After twenty-five books published, Mallory is still amazed and thrilled that she actually gets to make up stories for a living.

Mallory lives in Tennessee with her computer-genius husband and three exceptionally intelligent cats. She enjoys hearing from readers. You can write her at mallory@mallorykane.com or via Harlequin Books.

Books by Mallory Kane

HARLEQUIN INTRIGUE

738—BODYGUARD/HUSBAND*
789—BULLETPROOF BILLIONAIRE
809—A PROTECTED WITNESS*
863—SEEKING ASYLUM*
899—LULLABIES AND LIES*
927—COVERT MAKEOVER
965—SIX-GUN INVESTIGATION
992—JUROR NO. 7
1021—A FATHER'S SACRIFICE
1037—SILENT GUARDIAN
1069—THE HEART OF BRODY MCQUADE
1086—SOLVING THE MYSTERIOUS STRANGER
1103—HIGH SCHOOL REUNION
1158—HIS BEST FRIEND'S BABY**
1162—THE SHARPSHOOTER'S SECRET SON**
1168—THE COLONEL'S WIDOW?**
1180—CLASSIFIED COWBOY
1203—HER BODYGUARD
1237—DOUBLE-EDGED DETECTIVE‡‡
1243—THE PEDIATRICIAN'S PERSONAL PROTECTOR‡‡
1275—BABY BOOTCAMP
1300—DETECTIVE DADDY
1351—PRIVATE SECURITY‡‡
1356—DEATH OF A BEAUTY QUEEN‡‡
1416—STAR WITNESS‡‡

*Ultimate Agents
**Black Hills Brotherhood
‡‡The Delancey Dynasty

CAST OF CHARACTERS

Harte Delancey—This prosecutor finds that battling a deadly enemy and a savage storm to keep his star witness safe is easier than battling his growing feelings for her.

Danielle Canto—She's afraid of nothing—except storms. Forced to flee her grandfather's murderer, she trusts Harte to protect her from the storm and the murderer. But who can protect her heart from him?

Freeman Canto—The elderly congressman fought against illegal imports and drug-dealing through the Port of New Orleans, until his violent death.

Vinson Akers—This D.A. has tried for years to put Ernest Yeoman in prison. Now he has an excellent chance, if his prosecutor and their witness survive until trial.

Ernest Yeoman—The importer and owner of Hasty Mart convenience stores is rumored to have congressmen in his pocket. Did he kill Freeman Canto to keep Port of New Orleans tariffs and security low? Or is he just an innocent businessman?

Myron Stamps—The senior senator is implicated in Freeman Canto's death. Is he an innocent patsy or part of Yeoman's smuggling ring?

Paul Guillame—Harte's cousin on his grandmother's side is Myron Stamps's political advisor. Paul swears he knows nothing about Canto's death or Stamps's involvement.

Chapter One

Harte Delancey always felt like such a wimpy kid around his older brothers—probably because that's how they treated him.

He looked up from the grill where steaks were sizzling. Lucas and Ethan were tossing long spiraling passes to each other in the football-field-sized backyard of their parents' Chef Voleur home. If Travis were here instead of overseas somewhere, he'd be out there too.

Harte preferred more solitary forms of exercise—running, backpacking and biking. He chuckled wryly and flipped the steaks as Lucas made a spectacular leap and snagged the football out of the air.

"Steaks ready in five," he called out as his mom brought a big bowl of her famous buttermilk ranch potato salad from the outdoor kitchen to the already laden table. Lucas's wife, Angela, followed her carrying a massive casserole of baked beans.

"Everything looks great," Harte said.

"I hope so," Betty Carole Delancey said in her self-deprecating way. "The tomatoes don't look very good."

He eyed the plump, bright red slices with amusement. "If they were any better, the *Times-Picayune* would be on the story. What do you think, Dad?" he asked his father, Robert, who sat in his wheelchair watching Lucas and Ethan.

Harte's dad turned his head slightly. "Everything good," he said haltingly. It had been fourteen years since the massive stroke had left him partially paralyzed and unable to speak. With his wife's help, he'd relearned how to talk.

Lucas and Ethan washed up at the sink, arguing about who had the more accurate throwing arm. Then Lucas kissed Angela on the cheek before sitting down beside her. Ethan grabbed the chair opposite the two of them.

Harte took the last T-bone off the grill and set the platter down in the middle of the table. He sat between Lucas and their mother.

"Want to play a game of three-team touch later, Mr. Prosecutor?" Lucas asked as he tousled Harte's hair. Harte ducked but not in time. "Or should I call you *Monsieur* Chef?" he mused, stabbing a steak with his fork and holding it up for inspection.

"After you eat all that and can't move? Sure." Harte was used to Lucas ribbing him about his choice of career and his cooking.

Lucas was a detective with the New Orleans Police Department, as was Ethan, and Travis, an Army Special Forces operative, was stationed overseas. It was a sore spot with all three of them that their youngest brother had broken tradition and studied law.

As if reading his thoughts, his mom said, "I was hoping we'd hear something from Travis this week."

"What's it been—six months since you last spoke

with him?" Ethan asked, then washed a bite of steak down with iced tea.

"September," his dad said.

"That's right, darling," his mom said as she cut his steak into bite-sized pieces for her husband. "It's been seven months."

Harte saw Lucas and Ethan exchange a glance. He knew what they were thinking. It chafed them that their mother was so solicitous and gentle with her husband. Neither one—especially Lucas—had ever forgiven their dad for his drunken rages and punishing fists. It didn't matter to them that Robert's stroke had rendered him a docile wraith of his former self.

At that moment, the patio door opened. It was Cara Lynn, smiling and dressed in a casual floral dress that sported all the pastel colors of spring. Not that the north shore of Lake Pontchartrain in Louisiana ever saw spring…or fall for that matter. The weather was generally either hot and humid or chilly and wet.

Still, the sun seemed to shine brighter when their only sister and Harte's closest sibling was around.

"What a gorgeous day to have dinner outside," she said as she rounded the table, giving everyone a quick kiss, then sat.

"Nice of you to grace us with your presence," Ethan said, cutting into his steak.

Cara Lynn made a face at him. "I'm showing twelve pieces at the New Orleans Fiber Arts Show in just over a month," she said, "and I've got finish work to do on five of them. You probably won't see me again until after the show."

Harte's mother sighed as she set two loaves of French

bread on the table. "That's why I try to have these dinners as often as possible. Everyone's so busy these days."

"Speaking of which," Harte said, "the court date in the Freeman Canto murder case has been moved up. The judge will hear opening arguments on Tuesday."

"Tuesday?" Lucas said. "Five days from now? That seems sudden. Didn't you just take over the case a couple of months ago?"

"And they were talking about putting it on the docket for June. But now defense counsel Felix Drury has to have open-heart surgery, and the judge didn't want to put off the case another three or four months while he recuperates."

"Maybe you'll get lucky and Drury will plead his client, or at least try to wrap up the case early," Ethan said. "I've testified in a case or two where *Jury* Drury was defense counsel. He treats the jury like his own personal fan club. Plays to them and draws out his arguments. Plus, doesn't he love to file motions for acquittal?"

"Yes, he does. The D.A. got the notification about the new trial date around one-thirty today, and before three there were two defense motions on his desk." Harte speared a bite of steak. "So that means I probably won't have time to breathe until the trial is over, starting tonight." Just as he finished speaking, his cell phone rang.

His dad grunted. "Dang things," he mumbled.

Harte glanced at the display and excused himself from the table. "Got to take this," he apologized as he walked to the other end of the patio.

"Delancey? It's Mahoney," Detective Tom Mahoney said unnecessarily. The gruff detective didn't like cell phones any more than Harte's dad did. "Got a problem."

"What kind of problem?" Harte asked, smothering a sigh. Mahoney was an excellent detective, but he had a very broad definition of *problem*.

"Your witness in the Canto case was almost run down a little while ago."

Harte's scalp burned. "Dani? What happened? Is she all right?" He blinked away a disturbing vision of Public Defender Danielle Canto's exquisite body crumpled on the highway.

"Yep. A vehicle nearly sideswiped her on the sidewalk leading up to her house. Doubt it was an accident. The damn car left tracks in the grass—and skid marks—looks like it didn't even try to slow down—"

"Tom! What about Dani?" Harte broke in.

"She's okay. But real shaken up. Has a few scrapes and bruises from throwing herself up onto the porch, though," Mahoney assured him. "That saved her. The front steps are nothing but toothpicks now."

"I'll be right there."

"No need to rush," Mahoney said. "The excitement's over now."

"Well, it may not be the last of it. Did you hear that the Canto case has been moved up? It's due to start Tuesday."

"Hmph. That explains a lot. That car had to be sent by Yeoman. He doesn't want Ms. Canto testifying against him."

Harte agreed. Ernest Yeoman was an importer and distributor who supplied goods to all the Hasty Marts

in the Southeast. He had long been suspected of deal-
ing in contraband, specifically drugs, through his import business. "Please tell me you've got evidence that
ties him to this."

Mahoney cleared his throat. "Can't say. We picked
up some headlight glass fragments and paint chips
where the vehicle sideswiped the porch. We'll see if
the lab can match it up with a make and model."

"Where's Dani now?" Harte asked. "Did she have
to go to the hospital? I want to talk to her. Find out
what happened."

"She's at home. We've got her statement. You can
read it as soon as it's typed up."

Harte was already fishing in his jeans for his car
keys. "You left her by herself?"

"I told her to go to a hotel or a friend's house until
we could arrange something, but she's about as stubborn as her granddaddy always was. I've arranged for
a cruiser to drive by hourly through the night."

"Good. I'll head over there as soon as I find a judge.
The hourly drive-by is great for tonight. But I'm getting an order of protection. I'm not taking any chances
with my star witness."

THE BOTTLE RATTLED against the glass shelf of the refrigerator as Danielle Canto pulled it out. Her hands were
shaking. She tightened her fist around the cold green
glass with a disgusted huff. Her hands never shook.

But today was a special occasion, she thought wryly.
She'd felt the brush of hot steel and the prickle of splin-
tered wood against the backs of her calves just before
she'd managed to leap up onto the front porch of her

grandfather's home. She barely remembered doing it, but it had to be a new high-jump record. The wooden porch was at least four feet off the ground.

She'd hit the porch hard and rolled, bruising her thigh, scraping her knees and elbows and hurting her wrist. She'd rolled up to her haunches immediately, but between her aching muscles and the panic that had hitched her breath, she hadn't gotten the license plate. By the time she'd taken a deep breath and managed to focus, all she'd been able to see was the car's back fender as it screamed away in a shower of stones and mud.

She'd grabbed her phone and called 911, and waited without moving until they got there. She hadn't even considered inspecting the damage to the steps and the four-by-fours that supported the porch. Maybe she should check now, but that would involve getting a flashlight and going around from the back door to the front, not to mention the trauma of seeing how much damage the car had done to the porch. No. She didn't want to know—not tonight.

After grilling her for twenty minutes to squeeze out every detail she could give him about the incident, Detective Mahoney had guessed that the car had been sent by Ernest Yeoman. She shuddered. Could Yeoman be that stupid, or maybe that arrogant, to think that he could scare her into refusing to testify? A horrible thought occurred to her. What if whoever was driving that car had been sent, not to scare her, but to kill her?

She squared her shoulders. Whatever the reason for the attack, it was time for her to take action. She wasn't her grandfather's granddaughter for nothing. Freeman

Canto had taught her to take care of herself. She looked at the bottle of Chardonnay still clutched in her fist, then set it carefully on the granite countertop. Right now she needed a means of self-defense more than a drink. She held up her hand. It would not be shaky long.

Stalking to the bedroom closet, she took down the metal box from the top shelf and unlocked it. Inside was the lock-pick kit her granddad had given her for her tenth birthday.

"Never know when you might need to get through a door," he'd said.

The small leather case felt familiar in her hand and reminded her of the hours she'd spent picking every lock in the house, again and again. She didn't remember when she'd stopped carrying the small kit. Probably about the same time she started wearing lipstick and noticing boys. Well, she'd be carrying it now.

With a sad little smile, she set the case on the dresser, then carefully lifted out the other object in the box. Her grandfather's gun, a SIG Sauer. She wrapped her hand around the grip. The cold metal felt good against her palm. She supported her right hand with her left, the way Granddad had taught her, and slid her forefinger over the trigger.

She'd never shot anyone, hopefully never would, but tonight she was thankful that he'd taught her how to take care of herself.

She handled the weapon quickly and expertly, ejecting, checking and reinserting the seventeen-round magazine. Then she grabbed the second loaded magazine from the box. Sighting over the barrel, she nodded slightly. She wouldn't go anywhere unarmed until the trial was over. Next time somebody tried to run her down, she'd take him out—or his tires at least.

She took the gun, the extra magazine and the lock-pick kit to the foyer and put them in her voluminous purse, then hefted the bag to her shoulder for a quick test of its weight before setting it back on the table. She felt much safer with her granddad's things so close. Now she could relax. As soon as she double-checked all the locks. After a quick round through the house, she headed back to the kitchen.

Her hands had stopped shaking while she concentrated on cleaning and checking the SIG, but as she picked up the corkscrew to open the Chardonnay, they started quivering again. It took a couple of tries to remove the cork, but finally, she was able to pour the chilled Chardonnay with only a little clanking of glass against glass.

Holding the glass high, she said, "To you, Granddad. The bastards who killed you will rot in prison if I have anything to say about it." She took a long swallow and shuddered.

Grabbing the bottle, Dani walked to her bedroom, kicked off her high heels and frowned at the long scrape that marred the red leather of the right shoe. "Great," she sighed, and flopped onto the bed.

Outside, she heard a faraway rumbling of thunder. She shivered. She didn't like storms. They scared her. Her dad had died in a tornado when she was only seven. Until that awful night last year when her granddad was murdered, storms had been the only thing that scared her.

That night, she'd learned that home did not always

represent safety, that faceless monsters could murder a man without conscience and that as strong and capable as she'd always thought she was, she'd been helpless to save her granddad. But at least Ernest Yeoman, the man who she was convinced was behind her granddad's murder, would soon be brought to trial.

According to Harte Delancey, the prosecutor who'd been assigned to her case, the D.A. was practically salivating at the chance to get his hands on the suspected drug smuggler. Yeoman had long been suspected of using his import business to smuggle contraband and drugs into the country through the Port of New Orleans. He was also rumored to have friends in the legislature. Some rumors had even suggested that Freeman Canto was one of those friends.

Dani felt the determination that had sustained her since the night her grandfather had died rise inside her, pushing away the fear. She was not going to let Yeoman or anyone else frighten her away, no matter how serious the threats. Nobody would smear her granddad's name if she had anything to say about it.

She held her glass up in a salute. "I'm fighting for you, Granddad," she whispered, her throat tightening. Just as she brought the glass to her lips, something made her stop dead still.

What had she heard? Footsteps maybe, in front of the house? Or had the rain that had been threatening all day finally gotten here? Holding her breath, she listened. There it was again. That was *not* rain. It was footsteps.

She didn't move a muscle. The rhythm and the muffled crunch ruled out the raccoons that toppled her garbage can at least once a week. Raccoons didn't make that much noise. This varmint was human. Her pulse skittered as the footsteps crunched on the gravel driveway.

It could be one of the police officers or the crime scene unit, taking more pictures before the rain got too bad. But that was doubtful. Detective Mahoney would have called her, knowing how shaken she was.

Whoever was out there wasn't sneaking, but he wasn't tromping either. She listened as he rounded the house and came up onto the back stoop.

Dani tensed, but to her surprise, everything went quiet. She set her wineglass down and prepared to get up, angry at herself for her apprehension. She was *not* going to let Ernest Yeoman make her feel unsafe inside her own home.

Finally, a staccato rapping echoed through the house. Although she half expected the knock, she still jumped. She slipped off the bed and tiptoed down the hall to the front foyer. She worried her lip between her front teeth as she eased the gun out of her purse. Drawing courage from the heft of the weapon in her hand, she stepped into the kitchen, gun at the ready.

The silhouette of a man was outlined on the window shade of the back door. The dark figure's shape didn't look ominous, but it didn't have the reassuring outline of a police officer's uniform and hat either. Nor was he wearing the cap and jacket of a crime scene tech.

She eased closer until she was about ten feet from the door. Raising the gun, she thumbed off the safety. Just as the silhouetted man lifted a hand to knock again, she snapped, "Who is it?"

The hand stopped in midair.

"Get away from my door!" she yelled in a loud, commanding voice. "Now!"

"Dani, it's Harte. Just checking on you."

Her pulse slowed as relief coursed through her. It was Harte Delancey. *Great.* She rolled her eyes. *Thanks, Mahoney.* She should have known he'd call the prosecutor who'd been assigned Yeoman's case three months ago. "Go away. I'm fine," she said irritably. "Go study your briefs or something."

The shadow shifted and she saw his head shake. "Yeah, ha-ha. I never heard that one before." He spread his hands, palms out. "Come on, Dani. Open up. I'm not armed."

She shook her head in exasperation. "Well, I am," she retorted. "Now go away. I'm not dressed."

"Sure you are," he said. "I can see your outline through the glass."

Muttering some unladylike words, Dani slid the bolt and unlocked the back door. As she turned the knob, she braced herself for the sight of him. As much as he irritated her, she couldn't deny that he was easy on the eyes, which made her very *uneasy* all over.

But when she swung the door wide, she was stunned. The Harte Delancey she was used to seeing was slickly handsome, from his perfect dark hair and expensive suit to his blindingly polished shoes.

But this was no slick prosecutor who stood in front of her now. His hair was tousled and flopped over his forehead. He was wearing a T-shirt and jeans. Dani did a double take.

The T-shirt was a worn and much-washed New Orleans Jazz Festival shirt from several years ago. The fabric stretched across his chest and shoulders and draped loosely over faded, very nicely fitting jeans.

She swallowed. Suits did not do Harte Delancey justice.

Harte cleared his throat and Dani realized she was staring at his—jeans. Her gaze snapped to his, her face burning with embarrassment. And there in his expression was the polished prosecutor she was used to seeing. His dark eyes were filled with mischief, and a familiar, knowing smile curved his lips.

She glared at him. "What are you doing here?" she asked, letting her gaze sweep downward and back up.

He pushed his fingers through his hair, dislodging droplets of rain. "Can I come in?"

She rolled her eyes. "Oh, sure. Why not? After you went to all the trouble to sneak around my house."

"Sneaking? I wasn't sneaking. I couldn't very well come to the front door like civilized folks." He assessed her. "Are you all right?"

She shrugged. "I'm fine."

"You don't look fine. Are you hurt?"

She shook her head, suddenly feeling a lump growing at the back of her throat. Swallowing hard, she straightened. "I was just—thinking about my granddad."

Harte's brow furrowed and his snapping dark eyes softened. He started to speak, but Dani cut him off.

"I guess Mahoney told you what happened."

"Where did you get that gun?" he asked. "You shouldn't—"

He stopped when she lifted her chin. Then she realized she was still holding the weapon. She clicked on the safety and set it down on the counter. "I have a license," she said defensively.

He visibly relaxed. "Seriously, Dani. Did the EMTs check you out? Make sure you didn't break something?"

"I didn't break anything. The driver broke my porch." She had to suppress the urge to press her palm against her tightening chest. She just wanted to go to bed and pull the covers over her head. "What's the matter, Mr. Prosecutor? Afraid you're going to lose your star witness? I can guarantee you I will be there to testify. These *accidents* are nothing more than an inconvenience."

He shook his head, and his smile faded. "I'm positive I won't lose my witness." He pulled a folded piece of paper from the back pocket of his jeans and held it up between two long, sturdy fingers.

Her stomach sank to her toes. "Oh no. No, no, no," she said, shaking her head. "You didn't," she grated through clenched teeth. "Come on, Harte. Tell me that's not—" She reached for it, but he held it over his head. If she'd had on her four-inch platform heels, she might have been able to snag it, but she was barefoot, and therefore at least six inches shorter than he.

"It's an order of protection—" he started.

"No!" she broke in. "You are not sticking me in some airless bedbug-ridden hovel for weeks."

"It won't be weeks, and hopefully it won't be bedbug-ridden or airless." There was a definite tone of amusement in his voice. "In fact, you ought to love it. It's a bed-and-breakfast in a Victorian house in the Lower Garden District."

Dani crossed her arms. "I won't go. The public defender's office is shorthanded as it is. I have cases and trial dates."

"Your cases are more important to you than your safety?" he shot back. "Than your *life?*"

She blinked. "My life?" she echoed. "I object. Assuming facts not in evidence."

He shook his head. "Mahoney told me about the car, and I saw what's left of your porch steps. If that vehicle had hit you, you'd be nothing more than a smudge on the sidewalk."

Chapter Two

"Ouch!" Dani said, cringing at Harte's words. "A smudge. Great. Thanks for that image."

"Come on, Dani. Another public defender can be appointed to take your cases until this trial is over. You are in danger and no, I'm not just worried about my case. I'm worried about you."

Dani sniffed. "Better watch out. Con Delancey will haunt you for consorting with the enemy."

He shot her an exasperated glance. "Our grandparents' feud is ancient history. And it was probably just for show anyhow."

"I can believe Con Delancey was posturing, but my grandfather always fought for what he believed in. That's why he was—" She swallowed. Why were her emotions so near the surface tonight? Even as the question flitted through her mind, she knew the answer was obvious. Because she'd almost been run down by a car.

Harte held up his hands, palms out. "I'm not suggesting anything different. I just need you to trust me, or I won't be able to keep you safe."

Trust him? She *knew* him. He would do anything to win, just like his grandfather. He'd proven that three years ago. Luckily for her, right now her safety meshed with his ambition. She sighed in exasperation and defeat. "When am I to be incarcerated?"

"Tomorrow morning. I tried to get you in tonight, but they're full. They're letting us have the run of the place for the next two weeks."

"Two weeks?" Two weeks sounded like forever. Then the significance of the time frame hit her. "Wait a minute. The trial date's been set?"

"Oh, I didn't tell you. It was moved forward. It starts Tuesday."

"Tuesday?" Dani said, shocked. "You mean as in Thursday—" She held up a finger. "Friday, Saturday, Sunday, Monday, Tuesday?" she continued, counting each day off on a finger. "But we aren't ready."

"I know. Tell me about it. Don't worry. We'll prep all weekend. Anyhow, the B-and-B has agreed that we can extend your stay for as long as the trial goes on. They're happy with the weekly rate we offered them."

"Weekly rate? As long as the trial goes on?" she cried. "No. This is not going to work. I'm going to see the judge and get that order vacated."

Harte gave her that smile again, the one that looked more like a smirk and made her so angry. "You can try, but ever since I passed the bar, I'm Judge Rossi's favorite nephew."

She had to fight to keep her jaw from dropping. Of course he had an uncle who was a judge. Of course he went to him for the order of protection. "So that's how you managed to get a judge's signature this time of night. Must be nice to have relatives who will skirt the law for you any time you please."

His smile faded. "I didn't skirt the law. I merely

called a judge I know rather than picking one from the phone book. You'd have done the same, Madame Public Defender."

"Fine," she said grudgingly. "You said it was a bed-and-breakfast? I guess that won't be too awful. Give me the address. I'll head over there tomorrow."

"It's on Religious Street, between Race and Orange. But as of—" he glanced at the piece of paper he held "—nine forty-three p.m. today, I'm responsible for you. So I'll pick you up."

"Okay, okay. Fine." She held up her hands in surrender. "Anyone ever tell you you're a bully?"

"Nope. Never." He cocked his hip to slide the packet back into his pocket.

Dani couldn't help sneaking a glimpse at the back side of the snug jeans before she stepped around him to open the door. "I'll see you tomorrow."

He reached over her shoulder to push the door closed, which put him way too close. She caught a faint whiff of something fresh and citrusy as she glanced up at him. She was going to have to get some higher heels. Not being eye-to-eye with him made her feel small.

"Hold it," he said. "Not so fast. I want to ask you some questions about what happened tonight."

"I told the police everything. Go read their report."

"Tell me just exactly what you were doing when the car tried to run you down."

Dani clenched her teeth. She'd seen that determined glint in his eye before—when they'd faced each other across the courtroom. He'd badger her until he got answers. With a defeated shake of her head, she walked over to the kitchen table and sat. "I'm really tired, so could we make it quick?"

"I've got no problem with that."

She rested her clasped hands on the table and stared at them. "I was late leaving the office. It was probably six-thirty, so by the time I got home it must have been around seven."

He nodded without speaking.

"I pulled into the driveway, parked and..." She paused. "I walked around to the front of the house to get the mail. The car just popped up out of nowhere. I heard the engine rev, but I didn't pay any attention to it until the sound kept getting louder and louder."

"Where were you when you realized the car was coming at you?"

"About ten feet or so from the mailbox." She wasn't happy about having to relive those moments. She'd been through them already, she'd had to answer questions about them twice for the police and now Harte was asking the same questions. She pushed her fingers through her hair. "Every single bit of this is in my statement," she groused.

"You'd already gotten the mail?"

"No. I was walking toward the box."

"So you realized it was coming at you..."

She nodded. "And I just ran. I don't even remember jumping up onto the porch."

"Sounds like it's a good thing you did."

She rubbed her wrist. "I do remember the landing. Did you look at the damage?" she asked.

"A little bit. I couldn't tell a whole lot in the dark, but

the front steps are basically splinters now." He looked at her. "Why? You haven't?"

She shook her head. "No. As soon as they were finished questioning me, I came inside, took a hot shower and tried to relax. Then I heard you sneaking around."

He opened his mouth as if to deny again that he'd been sneaking, then apparently changed his mind. "Did you see him?"

"See who? Oh, the driver?" She shook her head. "I barely got a glimpse of the car. The first thing I knew after I started running was that I was on the porch and my wrist and my left hip hurt. And my elbows and knees stung." She lifted her arm.

Harte frowned at the angry red scrape just under her elbow.

"I sat up and tried to catch the license, but the car was nearly out of sight and I couldn't make it out."

"Can you describe the car?" Harte asked.

"It was dark, maybe black."

"And the shape? The size?"

Dani closed her eyes. "It looked really big, but that might be because it was racing toward me."

"An SUV?"

She shook her head. "No. It was a—" She gestured. "A regular car. You know, a sedan."

"Have you ever met Ernest Yeoman?"

Dani shook her head.

"Myron Stamps? Paul Guillame?"

"Come on, Harte. I've answered these questions a dozen times. For the police, for the other assistant district attorney and now I've got to answer them for you? I'm tired."

"Humor me," he said. "I want you to answer as if you're answering on the stand."

Dani sighed. "I know Senator Stamps. He used to come over here a lot to talk to Granddad. They'd argue into the night. I'd make coffee for them."

"What did they argue about?" he asked.

"You know all this," she groused. "The docks. The Port of New Orleans. Granddad fought for raising tariffs and taxes. He was convinced that lowering tariffs would allow more smuggling through the Port of New Orleans."

"And Stamps argued against that?"

She nodded. "Sure. He was on Con Delancey's side."

"Lower the tariffs to boost revenue and create more jobs," Harte said.

"Not to mention creating more crime—smuggling contraband and drugs."

Harte frowned, looking thoughtful. "I've never understood that argument. Smuggling by definition is bypassing normal import channels."

"You're not that naive, are you? They smuggle the contraband and drugs in *with* the legally imported items. Sometimes inside them. Higher tariffs cut into their profits, and enforcing the higher tariffs means more port authority officers around."

Harte nodded. "I know the reasoning. So back to Stamps. You're saying he and your granddad butted heads on the issue of tariffs, even though your granddad's position had never changed? I wonder why."

"Granddad didn't like Stamps, but he was too polite to refuse to see him. He always said—" Dani stopped. As an attorney, she hated speculation and hearsay.

Harte would probably light into her if she started relating her granddad's opinion of Stamps.

"What?" he asked.

She gave a little shake of her head and made a dismissive gesture.

"Dani, tell me. Anything might be important."

"Even if defense council would cut me off in a heartbeat for hearsay?"

His eyes softened in amusement. "Tell me and let me decide."

"It could be considered defamatory."

"Then definitely tell me."

Dani covered a yawn with her hand. "Okay. Granddad said that back when he and Con Delancey faced off over the tariff issue, it was a gentleman's argument between two public servants who genuinely believed in their position. He had a very different opinion about Myron Stamps."

"Tell me."

"He was convinced that Stamps was doing it for money."

"Money? What money? Why haven't you told me this before?"

She shrugged. "Apparently, when he was first elected, Stamps was all for more stringent controls on the port. Then a few years ago he abruptly shifted positions. Granddad figured somebody got to him."

Harte took a small notepad out of his pocket and jotted something down. "Somebody as in—?"

Dani drew in a long breath. "I don't know. I hate to be rude, but I'm really tired."

He assessed her. "Sorry," he said. "I guess I forgot

that you had an exciting evening. Are you sure you're all right?"

"I'm fine. Just exhausted and a little sore. I guess I'll see you in the morning around what? Nine or ten o'clock? So you can incarcerate me."

He smiled and shook his head. "Nope. You'll see me earlier than that. I'll be staying here tonight."

"What?" She forced a laugh. "Right. Now, that's funny." She walked over to the back door and reached for the knob. But before she could grasp it, he was right there, his hand out, holding it shut.

"Stop that," she said. "Get out of the way. You need to go home. I've got locks. Those people are not going to do anything else tonight—if ever."

"You can't know that. There's no way I'm taking the chance. I told you. The order of protection names me as the responsible party. If you kick me out, I'll just sleep in my car in your driveway."

Dani regarded him. His strong jaw was tight. The irritating smile was gone and his brown eyes looked positively black underneath the dark brows. He meant business. She took a step backward and threw her hands out in a helpless gesture.

"Fine, then. Knock yourself out. I hope your car's comfortable."

His mouth curled up on one corner. "It's a Jeep Compass, so it ought to be."

"Excellent," she snapped. "I'm glad for you. Good night."

He started to say something else, but Dani lifted her chin and pressed her lips together. He inclined his head in a brief nod, shot that irritating smile at her one more time and left, pulling the back door closed behind him.

As Dani turned the lock, her hand shook. The fact that Harte was right outside her door, making sure nothing happened to her tonight, should be comforting.

It wasn't. All it did was provide an omnipresent reminder that, at least according to him, she was in grave danger.

IN THE DRIVER'S seat of his Jeep, Harte pressed the lever that slid the seat back as far as it would go. He held it until the motor whined, then stretched his legs. He had about two inches more room than he'd had twenty seconds before. "Guess that's it," he muttered. Then he reclined the seat back and wriggled his butt, settling in.

He'd bought the Jeep because it drove nicely in the city as well as on dirt roads and hiking paths. He'd never slept in it, but figured it shouldn't be too bad.

As he searched for a comfortable position, he thought about Dani. He hadn't expected her to actually banish him to his car for the night. That house was huge. There had to be at least one guest bedroom. Hell, she could have at least offered him a couch.

Still, he supposed he couldn't blame her for the way she felt about him. The first time they'd met in the courtroom, she as a brand-new public defender and he trying his first case as prosecutor. He'd reacted instantly to her tall, leggy, drop-dead-gorgeous body and eyes that caught the sun just like her hair. But she'd entered the courtroom shooting daggers from those whiskey-colored eyes.

She was undeniably Freeman Canto's granddaughter. Canto and Con Delancey, Harte's grandfather, had both been fixtures in the Louisiana state legislature. And they'd clashed on every single issue, most notably the security and tariffs on the Port of New Orleans. Canto was fiscally conservative, while Con Delancey fought to keep both security and tariffs at a minimum to help the working people. And, as Dani had said, they'd conducted themselves as gentlemen. There had been a kind of honor among politicians back then. An unspoken agreement that while the politics might occasionally get dirty, the politicians would not.

The first time he'd faced Dani across the courtroom, Harte hadn't been completely surprised that she'd shown up prepared for battle, ready to continue the feud between the Cantos and the Delanceys. Her client, the defendant, had been a woman who'd killed her husband, claiming self-defense and fear for her life. But there were no witnesses, no evidence of spousal abuse and the woman had shot the man point-blank.

As Harte fought to win his case, he'd discovered what a great defense attorney Dani was. She was passionate, a dedicated knight battling for her client.

Ultimately, Harte won the verdict, but he'd lost the respect of his opposing counsel. Later he'd found out that Dani had appealed and gotten her client acquitted.

Once he'd gotten more experience under his belt, he'd had to admit she was right. That first case had been a win for him, but it was a Pyrrhic victory. It had taken him a few years and more than a few cases to live down convicting a battered wife.

Their paths hadn't crossed but a couple of times since then, which had helped keep the instantaneous attraction he'd felt for her the first time he'd seen her at bay. But he'd never forgotten how she'd looked when she'd walked into the courtroom that first day. She'd had on a short skirt and high-heeled shoes that made her legs look a mile long. He'd never forgotten her face, her body or the unconsciously sexy, confident way she moved.

But her body wasn't all that he'd found sexy about her. She was smart and quick. Across from her in court, he'd quickly found out that as a public defender, she was as tenacious and focused as a terrier.

A cramp in his thigh interrupted his thoughts and he realized he'd been nearly asleep. Rubbing the tight muscle, he considered the irony that he and Dani were on the same side this time. Well, sort of on the same side. She still thought of him as the enemy.

His cell phone rang. It was Lucas.

"How's your girl?" his oldest brother asked.

"My *witness* is all right," Harte responded. "How were the steaks?"

"Great, as usual. We just got home."

"Really?" He glanced at the time on the display. "Late night for you, at the folks' house."

"Not my idea. Ange and Mom were exchanging recipes. I watched a ball game with him." Lucas never referred to their father as *Dad*. "I'd planned to talk to you about the info you asked me about."

Harte sat up. "What'd you find out?"

"Not much. Nothing on the record. Yeoman's got a fairly clean file. Some small-time stuff early on, but he's managed to keep his record clean for the last twenty years."

"His record. What about what's not on the record?"

"Now, that's a different story. Every detective has an anecdote about Yeoman getting away clean while one of his goons took the rap."

"Yeah, that's basically what I got from Mahoney. There's got to be somebody out there that Yeoman cheated or framed, who'd jump at the chance to get back at him."

"I called Dawson the other day and asked him what he knew. I figured he might have run into Yeoman when he was chasing down Tito Vega."

"And had he?"

"Nope, but he made a couple of calls for me."

"I hope he's careful. This is the best chance the D.A.'s ever had to put Yeoman away. We've got to be careful about where information comes from."

"Our cousin's a good investigator, kid. He knows what he's doing."

"I know," Harte said. "I'm just worried. Yeoman's hired Felix Drury as his attorney. He's a shark. He'll eat us alive if we can't vet every tidbit of evidence we present."

"You're still not sure about Dani, are you?"

With a sigh, Harte rubbed a hand down his face. "I believe she's telling the truth about what she heard. It's just hard to take in and it's going to be harder to convince a jury. She's linking a respected legislator and a renowned attorney with Yeoman, a thug and a drug dealer. She says her granddad was certain that Senator Stamps was taking bribes to push for lower tariffs on imports. If I can prove that independently, and find a solid connection between Stamps and Yeoman…"

"Are you saying you're going after Stamps?"

Harte sighed and ran a hand across his five-o'clock—or midnight—stubble. "I don't know. I need something more than Dani's hearsay about what she heard that night."

"Well, Dawson's info may help. He called a guy he uses part-time—a former drug addict who's a C.I. these days," Lucas said. "Apparently, there's been talk on the street for a long time about Yeoman's connections in the legislature. Something else that nobody seems willing to talk about openly."

"That's all well and good," Harte said. "But the fact that nobody will come forward with solid information is what keeps the D.A. up nights. Nobody's ever been able to prove anything."

"According to Dawson's C.I., some folks think that connection is Stamps."

Harte sat up, feeling his pulse speed up. "Why am I just now hearing this?"

"Because I just got it. The C.I. said to check Stamps's voting record and his bank accounts."

Harte rubbed his eyes. "I'm already on the voting records. I've got an intern tallying his position on every issue under the sun. But I have no cause to subpoena his bank records."

"You could ask him nicely," Lucas said wryly.

"Yeah," Harte responded. "I could toss a pig off a roof too, but the chances of it flying are better than a Louisiana congressman volunteering private financial information."

His brother laughed. "I've got to go. Big day tomorrow."

"Me too. I'll get with Dawson tomorrow. I hope he's got something more solid than a drug addict's report of a comment heard on a street corner."

"Good luck with that."

"Yeah, thanks. I'm going to need it."

"G'night, kid."

Harte hung up and looked at the dashboard clock, although he already knew it was after midnight. As he shifted, trying to find the most comfortable position, headlights appeared at the other end of the street. Harte crouched down in front of the headrest and waited to see what the vehicle did. It slowed down, which accelerated his pulse. Then he heard a garage door open. Peering around, he saw the car disappear into a garage three doors down. He watched until the door closed, then breathed a sigh of relief and relaxed as much as he could.

His thigh threatened to cramp again. Thanks to his long, lanky Delancey body, the Jeep wasn't going to be as comfortable as he'd hoped it would be. Still, he'd appointed himself Dani Canto's protector. A little discomfort was a small price to pay to ensure her safety.

But damn, it was going to be a long night.

Chapter Three

When Dani woke up the next morning and stretched, she yelped in pain. Every inch of her body was sore, thanks to her crash landing on her porch floor the day before. Her shoulders were tight and painful, her right knee ached and she had a headache.

She pushed herself up out of bed and hobbled to the shower. Under the hot spray, her muscles loosened and the headache eased, although the scrapes on her knees and elbows stung like fire. She blamed the sore muscles, the scrape and the aching knee on the bastard who'd tried to run her down. She blamed the headache on Harte Delancey, although, if she were truthful, he didn't deserve it.

After he'd left, she'd gotten into her pajamas and climbed into bed, fully intending to drink enough to wipe his ominous words from her brain. But the wine's taste was bitter on her tongue. She'd tried to read, tried to watch TV, even put on a blues music station, but nothing helped. So she turned out the light and lay in the dark, feeling sorry for herself.

She missed her granddad. Sure, he'd been eighty, but he'd been as healthy as a decades-younger man. In fact, he'd been planning to run for another four years in the legislature. She had been planning to have her grandfather around for another four years and more.

It hurt so much that he was gone. She wanted this trial over and done for so many reasons. It had been over a year since the night he was murdered, but every time she had to talk to the D.A.'s office, the police or a judge, all the wounds opened up again.

Now Harte was putting her into protective custody until after the trial. *She* was the one being threatened and targeted. It wasn't fair that she had to be the one locked up while the murderers were free to go where they pleased.

Under the hot soothing spray of the shower, she felt the weight of sadness and worry, heavier than ever. To her dismay, her eyes stung.

"Stop it," she told herself. She never cried. To cry meant to lose control, and she did not like feeling out of control.

Turning off the taps, she dried off, then wrapped up in a short terry-cloth robe and squeezed the last of the water out of her shoulder-length hair.

In the kitchen she put on a pot of coffee. As she waited for it to perk, she couldn't stop thinking about yesterday and her near miss. It had been almost dark when she'd gotten home. As she'd walked from the driveway to the mailbox, she'd heard a car engine rev.

By the time she'd realized the car was coming straight at her, it was almost too late. Somehow, instinct had kicked in and she'd managed to leap onto the porch. The car ripped through the wooden steps and then swerved back onto the street and took off.

It had been a close call. Too close. She shuddered,

her shoulders drawing up. With a long sigh intended to help her relax, she poured herself a mug of chicory coffee. She added cream and sugar and stirred briskly, then took that almost unbelievably delicious first sip of the morning. It was so good it gave her goose bumps.

A few more sips and she felt her courage begin to rise. Coffee made so many things better. Consciously relaxing the tense muscles between her shoulder blades, she headed toward the front porch to see what kind of damage had been done. She stepped outside and breathed deeply of the cool morning air. March temperatures in south Louisiana could be as hot as July, but they could also be fresh and springlike. This morning was leaning toward spring. But she quickly forgot about the weather as she surveyed the damage. The car had taken a huge bite out of the front-porch floor. The steps were nothing but splinters, and if she hadn't managed to clear the edge of the porch with that desperate leap, she might be just as smashed and scattered as the wood.

Shuddering at that thought, she eased closer to the porch's edge. Had the car damaged the four-by-fours that supported the front end of the porch? She took another couple of steps toward the edge.

"Dani! No!"

The sharp words shattered the quiet. Dani jerked and spilled coffee down the front of her robe. She whirled toward the voice, her heart racing with shock.

It was him! She'd been so concentrated on the damage to the porch that she'd completely forgotten about his promise to sleep in the driveway. "Stop!" he shouted.

Fury burned the shock right out of her. "You!" she

cried indignantly, flicking drops of sticky coffee off her fingers.

"Don't move!" He held up his hands in a stop gesture.

But she had no intention of budging. He was approaching fast and she was four feet above him on the porch in nothing but a bathrobe that came to midthigh—maybe. No underwear. *Oh, brother.* Her face grew warm.

"Don't come any closer!" she cried out. When he didn't stop, she screeched, "Don't!"

He stopped, looking bewildered. "What's wrong?"

"Go around back," she said, gesturing with her head. She didn't dare move anything else. Her left hand pressed the front hem of the robe against her thighs. "Go."

Harte cocked his head quizzically, then shrugged. "I will, but not until you back up carefully toward the door. The front of the porch is sagging."

"No! You first," she insisted. Her ears burned, she was so embarrassed. "Please," she begged.

His brows raised and that damnable smile appeared on his lips. "Ah," he said, his tone lightening. "Okay, I'll go. But you meet me at the door in five seconds flat or I'll come in and get you." He gave her a brief nod. "Nice robe."

She glared at him, but she still didn't dare to move a muscle.

"Go to hell," she said.

He waved a hand and headed around back.

Dani baby-stepped backward until she'd made it through the door. Then she sprinted into her bedroom to get dressed, marveling at the fact that he really had slept in his car in her driveway. The idea that he'd actually followed through with it, in some sort of quixotic effort to protect her, gave her a sense of security she hadn't felt since the night her grandfather had died.

As Harte waited at the back door for Dani to let him in, he chuckled. Once he'd been sure she wasn't going any closer to the rickety front edge of the porch, he'd paused for a second to admire those amazing legs. As he enjoyed them, she'd squirmed and turned red. When she begged him to go around to the back door while nervously tugging at the bottom of the short robe, it dawned on him why she was so reluctant for him to leap to her rescue.

She had nothing on under the robe. That thought had sent urgent, almost painful signals to his groin, signals that hadn't faded yet. He clamped his jaw against the sharp, pleasurable thrumming and forced himself to think about something miserable, like hiking in a freezing rain—or sleeping in his car. It helped a little.

He pushed his fingers through his hair and rubbed his stubbled jaw, as if that would help wipe away the sight of those forever legs. He busied himself with smoothing out the wrinkles in his T-shirt. Just as he tugged the tail down, Dani opened the door.

She'd thrown on jeans and a long-sleeved T-shirt, along with a *don't you dare mention my robe* glare. "Don't you have a home to go to?" she groused.

"Morning," he said cheerily, then pointed vaguely toward the front of the house. "Mind if I…?"

She stepped back from the door. "Down the hall on the right."

By the time he got back to the kitchen, he felt a whole lot better. He'd found a glass and some mouthwash in the hall bathroom, as well as a comb.

Dani was sitting at the kitchen table with a fresh mug of coffee in front of her. She nodded toward the coffeepot. "Mugs are in the cabinet above. Sugar's in the white canister. Cream is—"

"Let me guess," he broke in. "In the refrigerator. That's okay. I take it black." He retrieved a mug and filled it with the dark, strong brew.

"Of course you do," she muttered. When he sat, she looked pointedly at his wrinkled T-shirt. "Don't let me keep you. It's obvious you need to go home and get ready for work. I do."

"No," Harte replied, setting down his mug. "You've got to get ready to go to the bed-and-breakfast. Pack enough for at least two weeks."

Her mug stopped an inch from her lips. "I told you last night. I can't be away from work that long. I've got my own cases, people depending on me."

He drew in a frustrated breath. "Listen, Dani. This is your grandfather's murder trial. Your testimony is vital to link Ernest Yeoman directly to your granddad's murder. Do you have any idea how long the D.A.'s office has been trying to get something concrete on him?"

"You've got fingerprints from that night, right?"

"Not Yeoman's. He's got more sense than to show up at a crime scene." He looked at her quizzically. "Didn't anyone tell you about the fingerprinting results? There was one good set. They belong to a small-time burglar and general no-count named Chester Kirkle. He's got two convictions and he's on parole now. He's not going to make the most reliable witness. Our best bet is to talk him into giving up Yeoman. Then his testimony, boosted by yours about what they said, should put Yeoman away for conspiracy to commit assault with intent."

"Not murder?"

"I'm going to try for conspiracy to commit murder, but you know how unlikely we are to get it. Yeoman has an excellent alibi for the time frame."

"I know," she said, shaking her head. "I know. What are the chances this Kirkle will give Yeoman up?"

"I think once the trial date is set and he's looking at his third strike on top of parole violation, he'll flip."

She looked thoughtful. "And when he testifies against Yeoman, then Yeoman goes down too?"

"That's the plan," Harte agreed, "*if* Kirkle makes a credible witness and the jury believes that Yeoman sent him and the others to threaten your grandfather."

"Can you prove it's Yeoman who's trying to run me down?"

"I think so. I think it will be fairly easy to show him as a thug who hires thugs," Harte continued. "It matches his style."

She ducked her head and took a sip of coffee. "Beating an old man to death," she muttered.

When she looked up, Harte was surprised to see a shimmer of dampness in her eyes. The two times he'd talked to her over the past three months since he'd been appointed to the case, she'd been determined and angry about her grandfather's murder. Not once had he seen even the hint of a tear.

"Okay," she said, straightening. "I'll do whatever I have to."

He was absolutely sure that was true. The spark in her golden brown eyes spoke of the kind of person she was. If she wanted something, she went after it. She didn't sit back and wait. It wasn't in her nature.

"Look at the bright side. It's possible the trial could even be over in a few days."

She eyed him narrowly. "You don't really believe that, do you?"

He shrugged, being truthful. "No one knows anything for sure until it starts. But I can promise you this. Until the trial is over and Yeoman is in prison, you are in danger and it's my responsibility to keep you safe."

"Thank you," Dani said grudgingly.

"Have you heard who defense counsel is? Felix Drury."

"Jury Drury? I've heard he's been known to list dozens of potential witnesses on his intent-to-call list." Drury was one of the best-known defense attorneys in Orleans Parish. He was known for his ruthlessness, cleverness and charm. He'd defended some very famous and very infamous people.

Harte nodded. "He's a shark."

"Can you limit the number of witnesses he can call?"

"There's not much case law on limiting the number of witnesses," Harte said. "All I can do is discredit them or object if he tries to parade too many character witnesses in front of the jury. Of course, even if he doesn't bombard us with witnesses, even if he rests early, the jury could take forever to deliberate."

"I thought you were confident," she said, frowning.

"I am fairly confident, but there are problems. You didn't actually see the men, and you're the only witness to what they said. As you know, that can be construed as hearsay. Chester Kirkle is wavering. I think he'll roll on Yeoman. Until he signs on the dotted line, he's a wild card. So it very well may come down to your veracity versus Yeoman's reputation."

"Why is that even a question? He's a drug dealer and I'm a public defender."

"He owns twenty-three Hasty Mart convenience stores in the New Orleans area. On paper, he's a fine, upstanding businessman who made a couple of mistakes in his youth. He's known for his substantial political contributions as well as community support. And he's never been arrested as an adult," Harte said.

"Oh my gosh, the way you're talking, he sounds a lot more like a model citizen than a thug. We've probably already lost."

"Not if I can help it. I've got some feelers out about his connection with Stamps and Paul Guillame."

Dani groaned as she rose to put her mug in the sink. "So the trial could last from one day to forever. Please don't make me stay locked up until the trial is over. Why can't the police officers babysit me here?"

Harte stood too. He reached around her to set his mug down, and immediately regretted it. It put his nose way too close to her hair, which smelled like strawberries and sunshine. He backed up. "You know the answer to that," he said, his voice a bit husky from reaction.

"They know where I live," Dani responded, hoping the flutter in her pulse wasn't evident in her voice. Thank goodness he'd backed away. He'd been way too close to her as he set his mug in the sink. His arm brushing hers along with his warm breath against her hair had sent a thrill through her, a thrill she didn't welcome. She thought she'd gotten over this little crush, or whatever it was. After all, even though she'd been wildly attracted to him from the first moment she'd met him as opposing counsel, she'd quickly seen how pompous and arrogant he was, with his custom suits and his designer briefcase.

She turned toward him, forcing her mind back to the problem at hand. "How long do I have to get ready?"

"Go pack. I'll wash the mugs and the coffeepot. You can call the newspaper and the post office from the B-and-B."

"This is *so* inconvenient," she whined as she turned on her heel.

"Not as inconvenient as getting yourself killed," Harte shot after her.

TWO HOURS LATER Dani pulled the crisscross strap of her purse off over her head and tossed it onto the white bedspread patterned with roses and lovebirds as Harte rolled her suitcase into the room. The entire bedroom was decorated in cluttered Victorian, just like the living room she'd just walked through. Frilly, lacy white curtains graced the windows, and every surface was covered with doilies, vases of silk flowers and filigreed photo frames.

The room was much too girlie for her taste. It was beautiful and she certainly appreciated pretty feminine things, but she limited the lace and frills to her underwear. She preferred her clothes tailored and her furnishings and décor sparse and open.

"Ugh," she groaned.

"What?" Harte said. "Is something wrong?"

She swept the air with her hand. "You tell me. Do I look like the type who would live among roses and lace?" She winced as she remembered the pink lacy panties and bra she'd donned this morning.

His gaze sharpened as if he were activating X-ray vision.

"That was a rhetorical question," she said archly. "Why am I on the first floor? Wouldn't I be harder to get to upstairs?"

Harte was still looking at her.

"That one *wasn't* rhetorical," she said.

He blinked and met her gaze. "Yeah, you'd be harder to get to, but also harder to get *out*. I don't want you stuck with no means of escape."

She frowned. "Means of escape? Really? I thought the reason you brought me here was so they won't know where I am."

He nodded. "That's true. But it's possible that someone could follow me or the police officers."

She knew she had to have a police babysitter, but him? "You?"

"I've got to prep you for your testimony. And since we're paying for this lovely place, we might as well use it. Besides, I don't want you traveling back and forth to my office—or my home." His mouth curved up in a quick, crooked smile, different from the knowing smirk he usually sent her way. It was a little comical and very charming.

Charming? *Where had that come from?* Dani shook her head.

"What?" Harte asked.

"What?" she retorted.

"You were shaking your head."

"No, I wasn't," she muttered as she grabbed her suitcase and hefted it up onto the cedar chest that sat at the foot of the bed. "I guess I've got to unpack."

"I guess you do, if you've finally accepted that you're stuck here. I can promise you that a knight in shining armor is not going to sweep in and save you from protective custody."

"A girl can dream," she said on a sigh as she unzipped the case. Her makeup kit and hairbrush were on top. She picked them up and started toward the bathroom, then turned back and looked at Harte.

"So, are *you* taking the first shift?"

"No. I'm waiting to hear from Captain Mahoney, letting me know who he's sending over. I'll stay here until they get here."

Dani straightened and propped her hands on her hips. "I don't like this. You are way too serious. Shouldn't I be somewhere farther away? Like maybe Seattle? If you're that worried about them figuring out where I am." She expected him to say no, that he was just taking precautions, but he didn't.

That worried her.

"It's possible they were just trying to scare you, but from the looks of your front steps, I'd say if you hadn't managed to jump onto the porch, you might be in the hospital, or—"

"Do *not* say smudge on the sidewalk again. I get the

picture. So when—?" she had started to ask when his cell phone interrupted her.

He held up a finger as he fished it out of his jacket pocket and answered it. "Delancey," he said shortly, turning toward the picture window as he listened. "Hello? Hello?" He walked closer to the window. "Mr. Akers, I can hardly hear you. Hold on." He looked at the phone's display and muttered, "What's with the bad reception? It was fine the other day." He stepped into the living room.

Vincent Akers was the district attorney. Dani could hear Harte trying to talk with him. After a moment, she heard him utter a mild curse, and then he appeared in the bedroom doorway. "The cell service here sucks," he said irritably, pocketing his phone. "Your day-shift officer just pulled up. I'll get you two introduced and then I need to take off." He glanced at his watch. "I've got a meeting with the D.A., I think."

"Should you call back on the B-and-B's phone and check?"

"Nah, by that time I could be halfway to his office."

"Speaking of offices, when can I get some things from mine?" she asked. "My desk is full of stuff I have to read and reports and briefs I need to write."

"I told you, the public defender's office will assign your cases to someone else. You need to worry about staying safe."

"That's all well and good, but even if somebody picks up my caseload, I still have paperwork to complete. I brought my laptop. I need that stuff."

"Okay. I'll ask the officer to take you to pick them

up. One hour, no more. And that's the last time you leave this B-and-B until I say so. Got it?"

"Yes, sir, Mr. Prosecutor, sir," she said, not even trying to hide the irritation in her voice. She heard the tinkle of the bell over the front door and sturdy footsteps approaching.

Harte turned and took a step backward. "I'm Harte Delancey."

"Field, sir," the officer said, coming into view at the bedroom door. "Ronald Field, reporting for protection duty." He stood straight and solemn, his right hand resting on the butt of his gun.

He was a medium-height officer with medium-brown hair and a medium build. He was pleasant-looking, but he didn't look as if he could do any better job of protecting her than she could herself. He wasn't in uniform, but even so, he looked spit-and-polished, from his crisply ironed shirt all the way down to his mirror-shined shoes.

As a public defender, she was no stranger to the police. But the sight of Officer Field standing in the doorway of the frilly Victorian room looking so earnest and official, despite his street clothes, and knowing he was there to spend eight or ten or however many hours every day guarding her, sent a frisson of fear down her spine.

"This is Danielle Canto," Harte said, gesturing toward her.

"Yes, sir." Field regarded Dani with a slight nod. "Ma'am. I know you, at least in the hall. I've been the arresting officer on a couple of cases you've defended."

"Oh, of course," Dani said, although she didn't recognize him. She felt her cheeks begin to warm in embarrassment. "Nice to see you, Officer."

"Thank you, ma'am."

She smiled. "Please call me Dani." She held out her hand and Field took it. He was nice, only a few years older than she.

She listened as Harte laid out the ground rules to Field about taking Dani to the courthouse to retrieve her papers—nowhere but her office, only as many papers as fit in one box or briefcase, straight back to the B & B.

"Take a different route each way and make sure you're not followed," he said. Then with a quick glance at her, he added, "And she's not to leave the house again."

She met Field's gaze over Harte's shoulder and rolled her eyes. Field's expression didn't change from quiet respect.

"Okay, then," Harte said. "Dani, be a good girl and don't give Officer Field a hard time, okay?"

She raised her eyebrows, wishing her superpower was shooting daggers from her eyes. "Watch it, Mr. Prosecutor. I could file harassment charges against you for calling me *girl*."

"You could," he said, amusement tingeing his voice. "Anybody can file suit, but it would be dismissed as frivolous."

"I could make it stick," she retorted.

Harte's face grew solemn. "Seriously, don't give him any trouble. This is for your own safety."

Suddenly, the back of her throat quivered and she felt a twinge of fight-or-flight adrenaline course through her veins. "I understand," she said evenly, silently willing him to go away and stop trying to scare her. Because it was working. The image of the mangled porch stairs rose in her mind's eye. If the car had done that kind of damage to four-by-fours, what would it have done to her legs—or her body?

Chapter Four

"I'll call you," Harte said. "Check to see how you're doing. And tomorrow, I'll start prepping you for your testimony."

Dani nodded.

Harte headed out the door, pulling a key ring with two keys on it from his pocket. "Officer? Walk me out, will you?" he said as he passed Field. "These are duplicate keys to the front and back doors. I'm giving you one and keeping one myself. You and the second-shift officer will exchange keys. One of you will be here with Ms. Canto at all times."

"Yes, sir," Field said, turning on his polished heel to follow him.

Imperious. That was it. She'd been searching for just the right word to describe Harte Delancey. And *imperious* was perfect. He was arrogant too, and she didn't like him at all. Forget how very nice he'd looked this morning in old worn jeans and a faded T-shirt with his hair tousled from sleeping in his car and his jaw shadowed by morning stubble. Forget how easy it was to imagine that he would look just like that after they spent the night…

You are so not going there, she admonished herself,

even as she pushed the curtains aside with two fingers and watched him fold his long, lean body into his car and drive away.

She wondered why an attorney in New Orleans drove a Jeep. But it did suit him, like the jeans and T-shirt and, she had to admit, the stubble.

"Ms. Canto?"

She jumped and let the curtains drop into place. "What? Oh yes, Officer Field." She hadn't heard him come back inside.

"Do you need anything?"

She gave him her sweetest smile. "Only a ride to the courthouse."

"If you're ready to go, my car is right out front."

"The Camry?" That was the only other car she'd seen parked in front of the B & B.

"Yes. I'm driving my own car. It's not a good idea to have a police car sitting out front all day and night."

Dani grabbed her purse, its extra weight reminding her of the gun and the lock-pick kit inside it. She glanced quickly at Field. Would he be able to tell she was carrying just by how the heavy bag swung against her side? Thank goodness Harte hadn't noticed. She slung the long crisscrossed strap over her head so the bag lay diagonally across her torso and rested against her left hip. Its weight reassured her. Babysitters or not, she wanted the feeling of security and control the gun gave her until the trial was over.

Looking at the back of Field's head as he opened the front door, she still wasn't sure he had what it took to protect her, if Harte was right about the danger.

Chewing on her lower lip, she wondered how easily manipulated he was. "I'm hungry," she said. "Are you?"

Officer Ronald Field turned to look at her. "Ms. Canto—"

"Dani," she said, still smiling.

"Dani. Mr. Delancey gave me my instructions. You can order something delivered later, because right now I'm driving you straight to the courthouse and straight back."

Dani suppressed a smile as she assessed him. So, Officer Field was more strong-willed than he looked.

Chapter Five

Harte stopped outside the door of the district attorney's office to finish speaking with his cousin Dawson, who owned a private-investigations firm. "Dawson, hang on a minute," he said into his phone. "Don't say anything else. I don't want to know how you plan to get hold of Stamps's financial records. I need to be able to use the information in court, so be careful, okay?"

"No problem. I'm working on an idea," Dawson said.

"Get back to me as fast as you can. I have a feeling the judge is going to set the trial date as soon as he can—soon as in next week." Harte's phone buzzed. He looked at it. It was Felix Drury, Yeoman's defense attorney. "I've got another call," he said.

"Okay, I'll call you back."

Harte thanked him before switching to his second call. "Hello?" he said.

"Delancey, why is my client being harassed about an accident that has nothing to do with him?"

"Uh, who is this?" Harte asked innocently. Felix Drury was better known as Jury Drury, because in front of a jury he was as charming and self-deprecating as Jimmy Stewart's Mr. Smith. In person, Drury was a self-aggrandizing, annoying grouch more reminiscent of Charles Laughton in *Mutiny on the Bounty.*

"Damn it, Delancey, you know who this is. Why are the police hauling Mr. Yeoman in? He was having dinner with his entire family at Commander's Palace when your client stepped in front of that car."

"Okay, Drury. First of all, she didn't step in front of the car, as you well know. I'm not going to put up with your usual blatant rewriting of the facts of the case. Got it?" Without waiting for an answer, Harte went on. "And why am I not surprised that your client just happened to be seen at one of the busiest and most prestigious restaurants in New Orleans at the time the vehicle nearly ran her over?"

"Mr. Yeoman and I are terribly sorry about her accident, as is everyone. We do hope she wasn't injured. It would be a shame for such a lovely young woman to be hurt like that."

Harte didn't like the way Drury said that. If he were paranoid, he might construe it as a veiled threat.

Drury was speaking again. "Now, you tell your boss to lay off Yeoman. It's bad enough he's having to endure the spectacle of a frivolous trial, for a murder for which he *also* has an alibi. This treatment of a respected New Orleans businessman is approaching defamation of character."

Harte glanced at his watch and sighed audibly, for Drury's benefit. "Okay, Felix. I'll give Mr. Akers your message."

"You're a punk, Delancey, just like your father. Both of you wish you were worthy of shining your grandfather's shoes."

Harte wanted to make a smart retort, but all he could think of was *Oh yeah?* So he just hung up. He opened the door to the D.A.'s office and spoke to the secretary as he passed her desk. He straightened his shoulders, then stepped into the Orleans Parish district attorney's office. He had no doubt why Vincent Akers had called him. He was probably going to get his butt chewed for securing the order of protection without consulting him. Still, he knew he'd done the right thing.

Akers was a micromanager, too controlling to allow his prosecutors to handle things on their own. He wanted to be consulted on and approve everything they did. And that chafed Harte.

Before he even stepped into the room, the scents of breakfast tickled his nostrils. Coffee, bacon, eggs and some kind of sweet rolls. The D.A.'s breakfasts were legendary. People would come down or up from other floors to sniff and place bets on what was inside the Styrofoam container.

"Talked to Judge Tony Rossi a while ago," Akers said without looking up from a form he was signing.

Harte resisted the almost overwhelming urge to check the shine on his shoes. He didn't move a muscle. "Yes, sir?"

Akers leaned back in his leather manager's chair and harrumphed. "Are you going to pretend that you don't know what he called about?"

"No, sir."

"Then stop standing there like an eight-year-old caught with a spitball and a straw and give me the details. Judge Rossi said you didn't fill him in much. I asked him why he'd sign an order of protection without getting all the details. You know what he said?"

Harte's throat was quivering with the urge to swallow. He couldn't resist anymore. He watched Akers watch his Adam's apple move. "No, sir," he replied.

"He said, 'That's Con's grandson, Vinnie. He told me his witness was in danger, and I trust his judgment.'" The D.A. folded his hands across his large stomach. "You know what I said back to him?"

Harte sighed. He was getting tired of this game. "No, sir."

"I said, 'If he's Con's grandson, then he's a smart-ass and a rounder, but you're right. His judgment is likely on-target.'"

"Thank you, sir," Harte said.

Akers shook his head. "No," he said. "That wasn't a compliment. It was a concession. I respect Judge Rossi. What I don't respect is you using your nepotistic connections to get an order of protection late at night without consulting me first. That is not the way I run my office." He harrumphed again and patted his stomach. "Is that clear?"

"Yes, sir."

"Do you have any idea how long I've worked to nail Yeoman? He's the slipperiest snake I've ever run into in my entire career. And I've seen some slippery ones."

"I'm hoping we've got him this time, sir," Harte said.

"You better hope we do. If he's brought to trial for murder and gets away with it, nobody'll ever be able to touch him again. Do you understand what kind of a predicament you've put me in?"

"I'm just trying to protect my witness."

Akers sighed exaggeratedly. "And it's not bad enough that we may lose our last chance to nail Yeoman, we're wading into deep alligator-infested waters with Ms. Canto dragging Senator Stamps and Paul Guillame into the mix." He peered up at Harte. "By the time this trial is over, my career's liable to be too. And if mine is, so is yours. Tell me what you've found out about Stamps's involvement. And while you're at it, don't forget to include Paul Guillame."

Harte winced internally. He had an urge to tell Akers what Dani said about Stamps, but it was no more than a rumor right now. If he could get something concrete, then he'd bring it to the D.A. "Don't have anything yet, sir," he said. "I've got somebody checking out a couple of rumors for me."

"Somebody?" Akers raised an eyebrow. "Would I be correct in assuming that this somebody is also related to you?"

Harte angled his head in affirmation. "I'm hoping that with the trial coming up, there's buzz on the street that could link Yeoman with either Stamps or Paul."

"And what if the buzz says that Yeoman's buddy was Freeman Canto?"

Harte swallowed again. Of course that was the simplest explanation. Yeoman sent thugs to beat up Canto because Canto was reneging on some agreement or had failed to do something. Forget Stamps and Paul. Even if Dani really had heard her grandfather's attackers shout their names as well as Yeoman's, it could mean nothing. But he did believe Dani and he did not believe the threats the attackers had yelled while they were beating Freeman Canto to death were nothing. He lifted his chin a fraction of an inch and challenged Akers.

"You know I have no more evidence linking Yeoman with Canto than I do with either Stamps or Paul," he said. "I've spent the past three months since you assigned me to the case trying to find a link while digging my way out of the avalanche of Felix Drury's motions and disclosure requests. We've got the fingerprint of a small-time thug named Kirkle on the doorknob of Canto's office, and I'm optimistic that he'll cut a deal and give Yeoman up. But until I have that deal in hand, all I've got is Dani's testimony. But there's got to be something from last night—a speck of paint, a sliver of a broken headlight—which can lead us to the car that tried to run Dani down. I just need one tiny crumb of physical evidence that links Yeoman to these *accidents*. If I can get that, I can make the jury believe that he killed Canto."

Akers popped open the lid of the foam container, increasing the mouthwatering smell of bacon and biscuits. "Are the police collecting that evidence?"

"Yes, sir. I haven't heard what they've found yet, but they're on it."

The D.A. opened a drawer and pulled out a stainless-steel fork and knife. "Fine. Now get out of here before I decide to take you off this case and make you bring Mertz or Shallowford up to speed."

"Yes, sir. There's just one more thing, sir."

Akers stared at him over his reading glasses. "What?" he demanded as he lowered the lid of the container.

"I just got a call from Jury Drury," he said. "He harangued me about the police pulling Yeoman in for

questioning about the incident with the car and Dani—
Ms. Canto last night. But that wasn't the main reason
for his call."

Akers's expression didn't change.

"He called to let me know that Yeoman has an air-
tight alibi for last night. He was with his family having
dinner at Commander's Palace."

"Of course he was," Akers said.

Harte smiled. "That's what I said."

"Get out of here."

Harte turned and tried not to bolt out the door.

"And, Harte," Akers said. "Try not to pull the entire
Delancey clan into the fray."

He nodded as he cleared the doorway. That wasn't
as bad as he'd thought it would be. His butt was still intact and so was his case. He had his uncle Tony, Judge
Rossi, to thank for that.

BY A QUARTER to ten that night, Dani had showered and
changed into pink satin pajamas and was sitting on the
frilly Victorian bed with her mini notebook computer
on her lap, working on a report that was due the next
day. A sharp rap on the door startled her.

"Dani? It's Officer Field. Detective Kaye is here for
the overnight shift. I'd like to introduce her to you."

Detective? It was protocol for the night-shift officer
of a female witness to be female, but it was rare that
detectives took protective detail. Dani set her computer
aside, got up and, after grabbing a white shawl to throw
around her shoulders, opened the door.

Field was still almost as crisp and polished as he'd
been twelve hours earlier. Standing beside him was a

woman in her early-to-mid-thirties. Her black hair was in a long straight ponytail. She was dressed in street clothes, slim tan pants and a green shirt that complemented her dark skin. The only thing that kept her from looking like a casual friend who'd stopped by to visit was the badge pinned to her waistband and the black leather shoulder holster. Draped over her left arm was a jacket that matched her pants.

"Hi," she said, offering her hand. "I'm Detective Michele Kaye." She had a firm grip.

"Dani Canto." She searched her memory. Had she met Kaye before? "Nice to meet you, Detective."

"Call me Michele," the detective said.

"Okay, then," Field continued. "I'm on my way. Y'all have a good night."

Michele glanced around the living room, then stepped up to the bedroom door. "I need to see your room. I want to familiarize myself with it." She shrugged, adjusting the position of the holster. The gesture was intimidating. Dani decided that Detective Kaye would have no trouble handling herself in any situation.

"Ignore the mess," Dani said. She'd had Field set the boxes from her office by the bed so they'd be within easy reach. Her clothes were draped over the dainty chair that sat in front of a Victorian writing desk, and her shoes were next to the boxes.

Michele snorted. "This is not a mess. My two kids—*they* can make a mess."

"You have two children? How old are they?"

"Seven and eight." She smiled. "My mother takes care of them when I work overtime."

"I didn't realize detectives were ever assigned this kind of duty," Dani said.

"I volunteer for overtime as often as I can. It comes in handy when you're a single mother." As she spoke, she checked the bathroom, then turned her attention to the bank of windows on the far side of the room. She frowned. "I don't like those windows. They're a security risk, so large and low to the ground. Someone could climb in."

Dani swung around and looked at them. She hadn't noticed how large they were, but now, with Michele's words, the nape of her neck prickled. "Wow," she said. "Thanks for pointing that out," she finished wryly.

"It's my job. But don't worry. I'll take a spin around the house every hour or so, just to be sure there's no one hanging around. This is a pretty good area. It'll probably be fine."

"Unless Yeoman, or whoever tried to run me down, figures out where I am."

Detective Kaye nodded. "That's why we're here," she said. "Well, I'll leave you alone. I see you're working." She started for the door. "Don't worry about anything. I'll be right outside. Holler if you need me."

Michele went out and pulled the bedroom door to, leaving it ajar. Dani tried to settle back down and finish her report, but she couldn't concentrate. Detective Kaye's critical assessment of the windows had made her aware of just how big they were and how close to her bed. She set the computer aside and got under the covers, then turned out the bedside lamp.

She was almost asleep when she heard something. She froze, holding her breath and feeling a creepy déjà vu from the night before, when Harte had walked around outside her house.

She was probably letting her imagination run away with her. *Settle down*. She didn't want to get a reputation as the public defender who cried wolf on her first night.

She turned over, trying to relax her tense muscles. She sighed, closed her eyes and did her best to clear her mind.

Then the noise sounded again. Like a scrape of a shoe on a hard surface. She yelped softly, then covered her mouth with her hand. She lifted her head and peered at the windows, trying to see if she could spot a moving shadow or something.

Then suddenly, a high-pitched screech rent the air. Dani shrieked involuntarily.

Almost immediately, a knock sounded on her door and it swung open. Michele stood there, her right hand reaching for her weapon. "What is it?" she whispered sotto voce.

"I'm sorry. Something made a horrible noise outside the window. But now that I think about it, I'm sure it was cats fighting," Dani whispered, feeling silly.

Michele walked over to the windows and parted the curtains to look out. "I heard the screeching. I'm pretty sure it was cats too. But get your shoes on and go into the living room," she said. "I'm going to take a walk around the house."

"I'm sorry," Dani repeated, but Michele was already heading out the front door.

Dani jumped up, shoved her feet into her sandals and grabbed her purse before going into the living room.

She clutched the bag to her chest as she waited for Michele to return.

When the front doorknob turned Dani stiffened, but of course it was the detective.

"I didn't see anything," she said. "Not even cats. There were no footprints on that side of the house, and I think there would be, because it's been raining a little."

Dani nodded.

Michele eyed her. Her mouth twitched. "I see you're all ready to go, with your purse and your sandals."

Dani's face burned. She probably looked ridiculous, but she wasn't about to tell Michele she was hanging on to the bag because of the gun inside. She shrugged and smiled wryly. "I'm not used to being scared of anything. But I'm kind of spooked, since the prosecutor has got me guarded by police. I apologize for all the uproar over cats."

"Don't apologize. I need to know if you hear even the slightest noise. Now go on back to bed. Everything should be fine. Like I told you, I'll make the rounds every hour or so. I'll vary it in case someone's watching, but I don't think anyone is. This B-and-B is in a perfect location for hiding a witness. At the end of the street, with a vacant lot behind it. Not much traffic. I think I'll talk to Mr. Delancey tomorrow about moving you to a more secure room, though—second floor maybe."

Dani started to tell her that Harte had already dismissed the idea of a second-floor room, but she thought better of it. She wouldn't mind seeing Harte tangle with Michele. Besides, she still liked the idea of being on a higher floor. Less chance that someone could crawl in her window.

Chapter Six

The next morning, Dani woke to the sound of voices. "Granddad?" she whispered, and grabbed the covers to toss them aside, but they didn't feel right. She stared at the material. This wasn't her bedspread. She squinted up at the filmy curtains hanging at the tall windows. Then she realized where she was, and why.

The voices were still talking, too low to distinguish. She frowned, listening more closely. There was a male voice. No, two male voices. And a female. The door muffled them so she couldn't make out what they were saying. Holding her breath and concentrating, she placed the lower-pitched male voice. It was Harte.

She groaned. Why was he here? One thing she knew—it wasn't going to be good news for her. Unless maybe they'd firmed up the trial date. She threw back the covers and got up, reaching for her cell phone to check the time. Ten-thirty? Wow. She hadn't slept eight hours straight since her granddad had died.

She combed her hair and threw on jeans, a tank top and a red, long-sleeved shirt before going to the door. Harte, Officer Field and Detective Kaye all turned to look at her. Field was dressed casually today, but the paddle holster at the small of his back ruined his careful suburban image.

"Good morning," Harte said, with that smile on his face. "We've been talking about you." This morning he looked more like the man she was accustomed to seeing. He was dressed in a gray suit, a snowy white shirt and a multicolored designer tie. He was clean-shaven. Mr. Prosecutor was back.

She shot a glance at Michele, but she couldn't read her expression. She looked back at Harte. "Should my ears be burning?"

"Michele brought up the obvious security issue with the windows in your room. We won't be moving you, but I'm going to have a motion-activated floodlight installed just outside your windows. It might be inconvenient if a cat walks across the yard and triggers it, but you'll know if there's anyone outside your window at night."

She winced at his reference to cats. Had Michele told him? "Great," she said sarcastically. "I'll have warning that someone is about to crash through the windows and kill me."

Harte gave her a hard look, but Michele and Ronald exchanged a glance. Ronald's eyes twinkled. Michele's face remained immobile.

"It's the best option," Harte said dismissively.

Dani threw up her hands. "Fine. Fine. You obviously know best." She looked toward the kitchen, sniffing the air. "I smell coffee, thank goodness. Is there anything to eat?"

"I saw bagels and sweet rolls in the refrigerator," Michele said.

"The manager isn't here this week," Harte added. "Since we took over the entire house. He told me he'd left some breakfast items in the refrigerator. I feel sure you can make do."

Dani groaned as she poured a cup of coffee. Harte Delancey might be easy on the eyes, but he was really hard on the patience. And the fact that she'd gotten a good night's sleep hadn't made him any less annoying.

Harte nodded to Michele as she left, then turned to Field. "How did things go yesterday? Any problem with Ms. Canto?" he asked, eliciting what sounded like a snort from the kitchen. He ignored it.

"No, sir. We went straight to the courthouse and back. We brought two boxes of files and papers back with us."

Harte nodded. The rookie officer was impressively earnest. Harte had no doubt that he would defend Dani's life with his own if necessary. "Want some coffee? Ms. Canto and I are going to talk about the upcoming case."

"No, sir. I'll take a look around the house and up and down the street while you're here."

"Good. Thanks."

As Ronald left, Harte turned to the kitchen. Dani was dressed in the same jeans she'd worn the day before. He hadn't missed how well they fit her long sleek legs and trim, curvy backside. They looked even sexier today. How was that possible? He watched her retrieve a sweet roll from the microwave and set it on the small table. When she looked up and frowned, he realized he was staring.

"What?" she said, jerking the chair out and sitting down.

He walked over and picked up her coffee mug from the counter and set it in front of her. "Forgot your coffee," he said lightly, then turned to pour himself a cup.

"I guess Michele told you about my silly reaction to the cats?" she asked as he sat down across from her. She cut a wedge of cinnamon roll.

"Yes, but I don't think it's silly. You need to tell her or Field any time you think you hear something outside your window. I don't want to take any chances with your safety."

"Well, thanks." She gestured with her fork. "These rolls are surprisingly good. You should have one."

He tore his gaze away from her and sent a half-hearted glance toward the package. What he wanted to have was a chance to taste the little dollop of icing off the corner of her mouth. He swallowed. "I came by to tell you that the judge called me this morning. He apologized for the trial date being moved forward. Said he'd put it on the docket last week, but he'd been out of town. I'm thinking Drury must have seen the date on the docket. If he told Yeoman that the trial was moved forward, that could be why Yeoman has been trying to frighten you. You should be happy that the trial is starting. The earlier it starts, the quicker it finishes."

"I guess so," Dani said. "But that doesn't leave much time for prep."

"Right. We'll be working on that all this weekend."

"But Tuesday—I'm not sure I'm ready," she said, setting her fork down.

"Of course you are. You know the process. It doesn't

matter that you've never testified in a trial yourself. You've tried plenty of cases. You know what to expect."

She shook her head, and a couple of strands of her dark hair fell across her face. She shoved them back with an impatient hand. "I haven't been..." She paused, then started again. "I haven't talked about that night with anyone—I mean, other than the police and someone from the D.A.'s office back when it happened. Whenever I think about it..." Her voice cracked.

Harte watched her. He'd sat with lots of witnesses as they talked through their grief. Violent death was a cruel and heartless way to die. It left family and friends not only grief-stricken but guilt-ridden, wondering if they could have done something to prevent their loved one's death. He always felt tremendous sympathy for those left behind.

But the feelings niggling their way through his chest right now were more than just sympathy for Dani as a grieving granddaughter. He felt protective of her. He had an unprofessional urge to hold her close and ease her pain.

No. Not hold her close. He hadn't meant that. He *didn't* want that. He was merely concerned about her safety and state of mind. He needed to make sure that by Monday, she could clearly and succinctly describe what had happened the night Freeman Canto died. That was all.

Her voice interrupted his thoughts. He tried to concentrate on what she was saying.

"It's funny. I was okay at the funeral too. But ever since—" Her eyes filled with tears. She blinked and looked down at her hands.

Harte leaned his forearms on the table. "It's no won-der that you're upset now. You were almost run down by a car yesterday. Not to mention being uprooted from your home, which you shared with your granddad until he was murdered. I suspect that hearing those cats last night was the last straw. You're in a much more vul-nerable state than you've been so far since your grand-dad died."

Her brows drew down. "Vulnerable state? You make me sound like a Jane Austen character. Trust me. I am not prone to fainting on couches."

He couldn't suppress a smile. "No, I'm sure you're not. Now, about the windows. I want you to pay atten-tion to the things you hear and see while you're here. *Nothing* that frightens or startles you is silly. Tell the officers. It's their job to check out anything that looks, sounds or even smells suspicious. I don't care if you call them a hundred times about cats fighting."

She gave a small laugh. "I promise, despite the sur-roundings, I'm really not a hypersensitive Victorian maiden."

"You're doing fine," he said, patting her hand.

Immediately, her expression hardened and she drew her hand away. "Don't patronize me, Mr. Prosecutor." She gulped a large sip of coffee and picked up the cin-namon roll with her fingers. "So, are we ready to prep?" she asked, then bit into the gooey roll, leaving a bigger dollop of icing on her lip this time.

Harte's insides ached at the sight of her tongue slip-ping out to catch the sugary frosting. She was fascinat-ing. Haughty as a runway model one second, stuffing her face like a college kid the next. He looked at a point somewhere behind her head and forced himself to ignore her unconscious sensuality. He swallowed. "We'll start this evening. Unfortunately, you don't have a lot of evidence to testify about. Not that your testimony is not important. Just the opposite. I believe we might have a chance to put Ernest Yeoman behind bars for the first time ever. I merely mean that your testimony probably won't take that long. Still, I want to make sure you're comfortable enough with what you're going to say that you come across as earnest and likeable."

"Why wouldn't I?" she retorted. "You know, every bit of what I told you and the police is the truth, the whole truth and nothing but the truth." She stuck her chin out defiantly, although since she was still chewing, it made her seem like a stubborn kid.

"Hey," he said. "I'm not questioning your honesty, but you know as well as I do that if a witness is nervous or too emotional, it doesn't matter if she's telling the truth. What matters is the jury's perception of her. And I want the jurors to see you as the grieving granddaughter who is bravely holding it together, even though her heart is broken."

"Wow. Queue the violins," Dani said sarcastically. "Think you can pull that off?"

Harte grimaced at her tone. "I'm not implying that you're not. I know how much you loved your grandfather," he said. "All I'm trying to do is—"

"Right. Save it for your closing arguments." She got up and took her dishes to the sink and turned on the water.

He sat there staring at her back. He prided himself on doing a good job of easing the pain of grieving loved ones, but somehow, he'd managed to screw this up. She sounded contemptuous, just as she'd been back when they'd faced each other across the courtroom as opponents. But he'd heard a catch in her voice.

He wished…hell, he didn't know what he wished. Maybe that she'd trust him to keep her safe and get her through the trial.

He looked at his watch. "I'm due in court soon. I'd better go." He stood and picked up his mug, preparing to take it to the sink, but she whirled and snatched it out of his hand.

"I'll do that."

He pressed his lips together. "Okay. I'll see you this evening."

"What time?" she asked, then shook her head. "Oh, right," she said sarcastically, "it doesn't matter. I'll be here."

"It depends on when the judge in my case recesses for the day. I hope it'll be by six at the latest. Want me to bring you something for dinner?"

She eyed him narrowly. "I've been craving jambalaya. And the best jambalaya in the world is Mama Pinto's."

"Where is that?"

"You've never had Mama Pinto's jambalaya? Oh, your mouth is going to thank you! It is seriously the best in the world."

"And it's—?"

"Oh, just off Tremé. It's only about three miles from here."

"Tremé? Seriously? You want me to navigate through the area where they're filming the TV series during rush hour? It'll take me an hour to get from the court-house to there and from there to here. And that's if Hollywood South is done filming. If they're still on-site, it'll be longer. I tell you what. There's a café that makes killer jambalaya about three blocks from here on Tchoupitoulas," he said hopefully.

"Okay, never mind," she said, her voice dripping with disappointment.

She didn't fool him. He knew what she was doing. She was baiting him. But that was okay. He'd virtu-ally imprisoned her. She had a right to a little revenge.

"I'll go to Mama Pinto's. I can't guarantee what time I'll be back, though."

"Get me some wine too, please. A good Chardon-nay. I'll leave the brand to you."

"Yes, ma'am," he retorted, and touched his forehead in a mock salute. "I'll see you tonight."

IT TOOK HARTE more than an hour to drive to Mama Pinto's, pick up two orders of jambalaya and get back to the B & B. By the time he pulled into the parking lot, the sky was dark with low black clouds. It looked as if any minute they would burst open and dump torrents of rain on the entire New Orleans area. As he reached for an umbrella from under his passenger seat, his cell phone rang.

"Delancey."

"Harte, where y'at? It's Dawson."

"Hey," he said to his cousin. "Just got to the B-and-B with a delivery of jambalaya for my witness."

Dawson laughed. "Lucas told me you've got a tiger by the tail with Canto's granddaughter."

"She's a little stubborn, but I've got it under control."
You wish, he told himself. "Got something for me?"

"Could be. My C.I. looked up a guy he knows who used to run errands for Yeoman."

"Errands?" His brain immediately took the single word and raced through the possibilities—loan collector, drug dealer, hush money.

"My C.I. armed himself with a newspaper that had an article about your upcoming trial and used it to start a conversation about Yeoman with the errand boy at a bar. He kept buying the guy beers and finally he opened up. He ended up telling my C.I. that the biggest part of his job was delivering envelopes and packages to an aide who worked for several legislators."

Harte's pulse went through the roof. *This could be it!* If he could connect Yeoman to Stamps and bring them both down, a small percentage of the corruption in New Orleans would be cleaned up, and Dani could feel safe in her own home. Not to mention that the win could catapult his career. "Well?" he said.

"Well what?" Dawson responded. Harte could hear the amusement in his voice.

"Come on, Daw. Did he say who the legislators were—and what was in the packages?"

"Nope. He didn't. But my C.I. gave me the errand boy's name. Well, *gave* isn't quite the right word."

"I'll pay you back. Just let me have it. This could be huge."

"I tell you what. Sounds like you're pretty busy with your witness, so while you're babysitting her, I'll have a talk with the guy and see what he's willing to spill and how much it will cost."

"Thanks, Dawson. But remember, anything you find out has got to be able to be confirmed. I can't use unverified information. I definitely owe you one."

"You definitely do." His cousin hung up.

It had started to rain while they were talking. Harte grabbed his umbrella and hurried inside.

What he saw when he entered surprised him. Dani and Michele were sitting at the kitchen table, mugs of coffee in their hands, laughing. They looked up in unison. Dani's smile faded and Michele set her mug down and stood.

"Hi," Harte said, amazed at how effectively he'd doused their good time just by walking in. "Don't stop on my account." He set the food and wine on the kitchen counter and took off his damp coat and tie. "Where's Field?"

"Today is his wedding anniversary. He left early and I'm covering."

Harte frowned. "He didn't tell me that."

"It's not a big deal, sir. One of us will be here twenty-four-seven."

Harte wasn't sure he liked not knowing exactly who would be here at any given time. He nodded reluctantly.

"I was just about to do my walk-around," Michele said.

"Take your slicker or an umbrella," Harte advised.

Dani and Michele both looked toward the front window.

"Wow," Dani said. "It got dark out. The weatherman said it was going to rain, but this looks ominous."

"Yep," Harte agreed. "I just heard on the news that

there's a tornado watch and a severe thunderstorm watch for the entire area. They're warning about hail and funnel clouds."

Michele grimaced and looked at her watch. "Mom was going to take the kids to a school play at seven. I need to call and tell her not to go out."

"That's probably a good idea," Harte commented, just as a low rumble sounded in the distance.

Michele took out her phone and looked at the display. "I don't have any service." She stepped over to the window. "Still none. That's odd. My cell service is usually excellent."

"Try the landline," Dani said, pointing to a table by the sofa.

Michele stepped over to the phone and dialed. She stood there a moment, then pressed the disconnect button, listened, then dialed again. Finally, she set the receiver on its cradle with more force than was necessary.

"That phone doesn't work?" Dani asked.

"It works, but all I'm getting is that fast beep, you know?"

"It means all the circuits are busy," Harte said. "Try mine."

"Thanks," Michele said. She took his phone and walked back over to the window.

Dani turned toward her bedroom. "I'll check mine too." She ducked into her room and then came out again. "How long is this storm supposed to last?"

"They couldn't say. They seemed worried that it might stall over the gulf because of a low front. If it does—"

Dani blew out a frustrated breath.

"What's wrong?" Harte asked.

"Nothing," she said shortly. "I just don't like storms."

Harte heard Michele talking. "Mom? Hello? Mom!" She listened for a few seconds, then handed his cell phone back to him. "Thanks, but you're not getting any service either."

"My phone's showing no bars too," Dani said, watching the display as she moved toward the window, then across to the kitchen area. She stuck it into her pocket.

"Your mom wouldn't take the kids out into a bad storm, would she?" she asked Michele.

"No, but it might not be bad over there yet, and I doubt she's been listening to the weather. She likes to play games with them, rather than just sit and watch TV." She looked at her phone one more time. "She heard me at first, because I heard her say *Michele?* She's going to be worried now."

"Harte, don't you think it would be okay if Michele ran by to check on her kids while you're here?" She turned to Michele. "How far away do you live?"

"Ten to fifteen minutes, but no. This is my assignment. I'm not supposed to leave my post until I'm relieved."

Harte felt Dani's gaze on him and tried to ignore it. He agreed with Michele that she shouldn't leave her post.

"Harte—" Dani started.

"Okay, okay." He didn't like it, but he supposed he could be flexible. After all, he was planning to be here for another couple of hours anyhow. Besides, he wasn't happy with the lack of cell service.

"I tell you what," he said. "As lead prosecutor on this case, I'm relieving you for one hour to go pick up a squad car. I'd like to have one here in case we have a problem. Even if we lose electricity, we'll have the police radio and a means of transportation that won't get stopped."

Michele looked blankly at him for an instant. "I'm not sure I understand—"

"Detective, you should pick up a squad car. If you swing by your house on the way, I don't think it would be out of line."

Michele's face lightened as his meaning sank in.

"I'll be here for a couple of hours. But don't delay. Try to beat the storm."

"I will," Michele said. She grabbed her car keys and headed toward the door. "Back in less than forty-five," she called over her shoulder.

"That was really nice of you," Dani said, sending him a smile.

"Yeah. Shocking, isn't it?"

"I didn't say that."

"Not out loud."

Dani propped a hand on her hip. "I'm beginning to think that this is not going to be a fun evening."

"Depends on your definition of *fun*," he said, gesturing toward the bag with Mama Pinto's on the front. "I rode all the way back here with the smell of the *best jambalaya in the world* filling my car. I'm going to eat. All I can say is it better be worth the trip."

"Oh, right," Dani exclaimed. She took the bag from him and peeked inside, inhaling deeply. "Mmm. That's Mama's jambalaya all right. Thank you," she said.

He angled his head. "Your wish is my command," he said solemnly.

"And I thought chivalry was dead," she murmured.

"I occasionally slay dragons too," he shot back as he picked up his briefcase and set it on the kitchen table. "We'll get started with the prep after we eat."

"After *we* eat?" she echoed, clutching the bag tightly.

Harte saw the twinkle in her eyes. First time he'd seen one there. It made them appear amber. He liked it. He wanted to see it again. "Hey, I got two orders, even though one looks like enough to feed a family of four."

Before he'd finished, she'd dug into the bag and pulled out the two cardboard containers. She shoved one toward him and opened the other, then dug into the bag again and tossed him one of the two plastic forks she found.

He picked up the fork, but he wasn't as interested in his jambalaya as he was in watching her. She opened the carton and dug into the mound of rice and shrimp and sausage. She shoved a forkful into her mouth and closed her eyes as she chewed.

"Best thing I ever ate," she mumbled, closing her eyes. "Mmm."

Harte swallowed hard. The look on her face made his mouth water, but not for food. A spear of pure lust shot through him. He was hungry for her. Grimacing, he forced down a few mouthfuls of jambalaya, then pointed at the bottle. "Want some wine?"

She looked up. "Will you help me drink it?" she asked.

He shook his head with a wry smile. "No. I'm working." Not to mention that he needed to keep his head clear around her.

"Well, I guess if you're working, so am I." She looked longingly at the Chardonnay, then turned her attention back to the food. Fifteen minutes later, Dani moaned and leaned back in her chair, stretching her arms over her head and arching her back. "Oh, I ate too much. Now I'm sleepy."

He tried to look away. He really did. But the red shirt had fallen away and her perfect breasts strained against the thin cotton of the white tank top she wore underneath, outlining her nipples clearly. He didn't think he'd ever met another woman who was so unconsciously sexy. And that was part of what turned him on. She had no idea how just looking at her affected him.

Shifting subtly, trying to tamp down his physical reaction, he reminded himself that she was his witness, and therefore his responsibility. He had vowed, to her and to himself, to keep her safe.

She caught his gaze and quickly adjusted her shirt so that it covered the revealing tank top, but her eyes stayed glued to his and something glinted behind them. Was it interest? Maybe even desire?

He busied himself with closing the cartons and putting them in the refrigerator. "Want a glass of water?" he asked.

"Sure, thanks."

He filled two glasses and held one out to her.

As she reached for it, a crack of thunder split the quiet. She jumped, nearly turning the glass over.

Chapter Seven

Harte caught Dani's glass just in time to keep it from turning over. "Hey," he said. "It's okay. It was just thunder."

"I know," she snapped. "It startled me, that's all."

He studied her closely as she took a deep swallow of water. Her hands were trembling. She really was afraid of storms.

"Are you going to be able to concentrate?" he said.

"Of course," she replied, her voice sounding slightly defensive. "Why wouldn't I?"

"If the storm passes directly over us, it could get nasty. We might lose power."

"I'm fine."

"Okay. That's good, because we've got a lot to cover."

"A lot to cover? I thought you said my testimony wouldn't take long."

"It won't. Not your direct. But with Jury Drury sitting first chair on the defense side, there's no telling how long he'll try to drag out the cross-examination. He's a master at rattling witnesses. He'll be on everything you say like a vulture on roadkill. Make you doubt what you heard with your own ears. I want to try to give you some defense against that."

Dani groaned. "As you pointed out yesterday, I've questioned and cross-examined my share of witnesses. I know what to expect."

"I know. But this time you're the one testifying. Keep in mind that your goal is to put away the scumbag who caused your grandfather's death."

"I'm not likely to forget that," she muttered.

Harte grabbed his briefcase and pulled out the Canto file. During the three months since Akers assigned the case to him, he'd familiarized himself with the specifics, including the autopsy report, Dani's witness statement and the transcripts of all the interrogations of suspects. Plus, he'd had the dubious pleasure of reading and responding to the mountains of motions filed by Drury.

But during all that time, he'd only talked to Dani twice. He remembered his dad telling him something his grandfather had said. *"Criminal law's nothing like television. It's ninety-nine percent paperwork and one percent court drama. So if you're in it for the limelight, find yourself another career."* Lucky for Harte, he didn't mind the paperwork.

"Okay. You pretty much know what to expect. So let's start with you telling me what happened. Start from the beginning, as if I've never heard it before. You've never testified on the stand, right?"

Dani nodded. "That's right."

"Keep in mind that facing a jury as a witness is very different from facing them as an attorney."

Dani bristled at Harte's tone. Now that he was talking about the trial and her testimony, he'd switched to his imperious prosecutor's voice. She didn't like it. It made her feel as if she were back in the courtroom, facing off against him.

Her immediate instinct was to shoot a cutting response at him, but it was beginning to dawn on her how hard it was going to be to sit in that witness box and talk about her granddad's murder in front of a judge, a jury and the man responsible for his death. So she bit her tongue and nodded again.

His brows twitched, but he didn't comment. Had he expected a retort? "Okay," he said. "Go ahead."

For a second, she wasn't sure how to begin. "I've thought about that night so many times you'd think I wouldn't have any trouble describing what happened." She rubbed her temple.

"Why don't you start with what you were doing that day?"

"Okay." She nodded. "That was the day of the City Hall Awards Banquet."

"That's right," Harte commented with a grimace. "The annual rent-a-tux rent-a-crowd."

"Exactly," she said with a smile that lightened her expression and put a twinkle in her eyes. "I was going, of course. I'd even bought a new dress. But I caught a stomach bug. I ended up throwing up all day. Granddad brought me some crackers and ginger ale—" She had to swallow hard before she could continue.

"So I'd finally gotten to sl-sleep—" Her breath hitched. "Oh, this is awful." Her fingers massaged her temple. "Let me start over."

"No," Harte said. "You're doing great."

She shot him a skeptical look. "Anyway, I woke up hearing voices." She shifted in her chair. "They were yelling. I heard one of them say, 'You'll do it or you'll regret it,' and Granddad yelled back, 'You sons of bitches can go to hell.' That was just like him. He didn't suffer fools gladly."

Harte nodded and smiled back at her. For some reason his smile made her feel better.

"I was groggy and weak, so at first I didn't pay much attention. I figured it was one of his friends and they were arguing about politics. That wasn't unusual. He had guests several evenings a week. I used to scold him about not getting enough sleep." She sighed. "If I'd gotten up then—" Her heart ached with a hollow, sharp pain.

"Hey, don't go there. Just stick with the facts. Stay on point. You're fine." He laid his hand on top of hers where it rested on the table and squeezed it.

She looked down, surprised at the gesture. It didn't bother her. Just the opposite, in fact. His large, warm hand felt so good, so comforting, over hers. She longed to turn her hand over and clutch his. She wanted, needed, comfort so badly. But she'd already discovered that she was much too vulnerable to his good looks. She pulled away.

"Watch out," she said. "The jury might think you're fraternizing with your witness." She aimed for a smile and a light tone. When his gaze snapped to hers, she realized she'd failed. She'd meant it as a joke, but now, her gaze caught by his, she felt something flare between them. Something hot and intimate. Much more intimate than the touch of a hand or a glance should be.

A flash of lightning and its accompanying clap of thunder made her jump, and that quickly, the spell was broken.

Harte withdrew his hand with a quick smile. "You're right," he said. "I'll have to watch it."

A chill slid through her—was it from the thunder or the absence of his warm hand on hers? She shivered and glanced up at the kitchen clock. "I wonder if Michele's made it home. The storm is getting worse."

A second flash and rumble proved her right.

"I'm sure she's fine," Harte said. "She'll be back soon."

Another time, Dani might resent Harte's carefully patient tone, as if he were trying to calm a screaming child. But right now he was her only port in the storm— literally. And he was being quite nice.

He pulled his cell phone out of his pocket and checked it. He shook his head.

"Still no service?" she asked. In the distance, a high-pitched wail signaled that emergency vehicles were responding to calls.

"Not even one bar. When I was trying to talk to the D.A., I had two bars and it still kept dropping the connection. I hope the storm hasn't knocked out any towers." He sighed and pocketed the phone. "So. Your grandfather and whoever was in his study were yelling."

She cleared her throat. "Then I heard noises—grunts and crashes, like furniture being knocked over or things being thrown. I didn't know at the time, but now I know they were hitting him. When I think of those awful sounds, I—" She stopped. She had to swallow a couple of times to get rid of the lump in her throat. "There was one guy. He was louder than the others, sounded like he was in charge. He's the one who started naming names."

"What names did you hear?"

Dani looked at Harte blankly for a moment. Her head was filled with the awful, sickening sounds she'd heard that night. The dull thud of fists hitting flesh. The crash of a body falling against a table or the floor. Sounds that would always haunt her dreams.

"Dani?" Harte said. "What names did you hear?"

"Yeoman, Senator Stamps and Paul Guillame. All that's in my statement."

"I know. But remember, I asked you to tell me about the night as if I'd never heard it before."

She sighed. "I heard 'Mr. Yeoman sent us,' and—"

"Okay, hold on a second," Harte interrupted. "One of the men said, 'Yeoman sent us'?"

"He said, 'Mr. Yeoman sent us.'"

"You're absolutely sure? It couldn't have been 'Mr. Yeoman said' or 'Mr. Yeoman should'?"

Irritation burned in her stomach. "You know it's not either of those. He said, 'Mr. Yeoman sent us.'"

Harte studied her for a moment. "Okay. Don't forget that I'm asking you these questions for the jury. What else did they say?"

"I couldn't understand everything. The next thing I could make out was something about Senator Stamps, and—" She stopped. Just like that night, the exact words the men had said eluded her.

"Can you tell me specifically what they said when they mentioned Stamps's name?" Harte prodded.

"They didn't *mention* Stamps's name. They yelled it."

"Okay," he said with exaggerated patience.

She closed her eyes and forced herself back there. Creeping quietly across the hardwood floor toward Granddad's study, her stomach queasily protesting, listening to the awful sounds and trying to remember where her cell phone was so she could call 911. "It was like 'Senator Stamps warned or armed or aimed.' I was groggy from nausea medication and terrified, because I couldn't figure out what was happening."

Harte's mouth thinned. "That brings up a good point. Where were you that night while all this was going on?"

"I was trying to get to the telephone in the living room."

"And where was your grandfather?"

"In his study, on the other side of the house."

"That distance has been measured. From the door of your bedroom to the door of Freeman Canto's study is sixty-two feet. Are you telling me that you could hear and understand what the men were saying?"

She bristled. "Ye-e-es." She drew out the word sarcastically.

"Dani, you're supposed to be answering as if you were on the witness stand. You're the prosecution's main witness. As an attorney you know better than to get defensive. Remember that it's your job to give the judge and jury an accurate recounting of the events that led up to your grandfather's death."

The control she was holding on to with such desperation cracked and her eyes filled with tears. "This is a lot harder than I thought it would be. I'm talking about hearing men beating my grandfather to death while I was three rooms away."

Harte's gaze seemed to soften. "It'll be even harder

when you're on the witness stand," he said gently. "How many phones are there in the house?"

"Besides the one in the living room, there's one in Granddad's study. Then there's my cell phone, which was in my purse on the hall table, and Granddad's, which I believe was in his pocket." She pushed her chair back from the table and began pacing. Her path took her toward the front room where the rain was pounding the picture window. "And you don't have to remind me that it will be harder. I know that."

Harte continued with his questioning. "Now, if you were frightened, sick and medicated, how can you possibly be sure the name you heard was Stamps?"

"I know what I heard. He didn't just say Stamps, he said Senator Stamps. And I heard the name Paul Guillame too and he's Stamps's political adviser."

"Again, Ms. Canto, you've admitted that you were medicated. In fact, you really can't testify to what the men said, can you? They could have said William or DeYoung or a dozen other names, right? It might not have been a name at all. It could have been anything."

Dani spoke clearly and calmly. "I was there, and I know what I heard. I can't tell you exactly what they said about Senator Stamps or Paul Guillame, but I am absolutely certain those names were spoken that night, along with the name Mr. Yeoman." She glanced at him sidelong. "And don't think for a minute that I don't know who Paul Guillame is."

"Objection. Irrelevant."

"No, it's not. Tell me, counselor, is it going to impact me that my attorney is related to one of the people whose name came up while my grandfather was being beaten to death?"

Harte's mouth thinned. "The D.A. has considered that and is not concerned. We're marginally related at best. He's like a third cousin."

"So Akers asked you about it."

"I'm your attorney. Don't even suggest that I don't have your best interests at heart. But please, by all means get all this hostility out before you actually go on the stand. And don't forget that it's not going to be me badgering you about what you heard. I'll let you tell the jury what happened in your own words. It's going to be Drury who'll be hitting you with the tough questions. He's a snake. Don't let him upset you. Think about what you tell your own witnesses. They lose credibility if they let the opposing attorney get to them."

Dani tried to compose herself. Everything Harte said was true. But the renewed pain of her grandfather's violent death, combined with the storm outside and the fact that she had to rely on Harte Delancey, her courtroom nemesis, was about to undo her. "I apologize," she muttered.

"Let's get back to the question at hand. Isn't it true that you're *not* certain about the names you heard? That you're merely desperate to find someone to blame for your grandfather's death?"

"That is *not* true. And of course I'm—" She stopped. Her breath caught in a sob. The tears she'd been trying to hold back stung her eyes. She blinked fiercely. She would not cry!

"Okay, okay," Harte said gently. He sat back. "Don't

worry about not being absolutely sure about Stamps and Guillame. As long as you're positive about Yeoman."

She sniffed. "But I am sure—like ninety-nine percent. About Stamps and Guillame, I mean. I'm definitely a hundred percent about Yeoman. That guy said his name twice, or maybe three times."

"Okay. That's good. When you're certain, be sure the jury knows you're certain. Now, go on. You said you heard violent noises."

She nodded. "They must have been hitting him. I heard him fall, and one of them said, 'Do you understand Mr. Yeoman's message?' But Granddad didn't answer. Then I heard them say, 'We better get out of here. The granddaughter will be home soon. And I think he's hurt—bad.'" Her breath caught again and her hand flew up to cover her mouth.

"It was so awful," she mumbled from behind her hand.

"Come back over here and sit down," Harte said. "Want some coffee?"

She shook her head. "No. I'm fine. I just can't help thinking of Granddad. They *murdered* him. He must have been so scared in those last minutes—" She stopped and tried to suppress the little sobs that kept quivering in her throat. "And I wasn't able to help him. By the time I got to his study, the men were gone."

"They didn't pass you as they left?"

She shook her head. "The study has French doors that lead to the outside. That's how they got in and how they left."

He studied her for a few seconds, then turned his attention to his water glass, tracing a finger down the side. He spoke without looking up. "You know, my grandfather was murdered too."

Dani was surprised. He didn't seem like the type to share his personal life casually. Certainly not with a witness—or a rival.

She nodded. "I'd heard that. He was killed by one of his employees?" She looked at him, expectant, but apprehensive. Was he about to try to give her encouragement by relating some anecdote about bravery in the face of tragedy? Or how Con's wife testified, head held high, even though she was heartbroken?

"He was murdered by his personal assistant, Armand Broussard."

"I've heard that name," she said. She waited for a few seconds, but he didn't explain why he'd brought up his grandfather. "What are you saying?"

He shrugged. "Just that we have something in common." He grimaced, then tilted his head. "I never got the chance to know him because someone murdered him. He died the year I was born," he said quietly.

"The year you were born?" Dani said. "I'm sorry. It's awful that you never got to know him."

Harte met her gaze, and his dark eyes, which normally caught the light like brown bottle glass, were soft and sincere. "What you've been through is worse. You had your grandfather with you for your whole life. I can't even imagine how much you must miss him."

One of the tears that kept gathering in Dani's eyes slipped down her cheek. To her surprise, Harte reached over and stopped it with a finger. She barely felt his touch, but somehow, it acted like a current of electricity, sizzling through her, creating heat in every inch of her. She stared into his eyes, wondering what he would do if she leaned over and kissed him. Then wondering what she would do if he kissed her back.

For a split second, their eyes held; then Harte blinked and cleared his throat. "So, do you think you're ready for Jury Drury?"

Dani moistened her lips. "I'm sure I'm not," she said with a tiny, ironic smile.

"You just do what the oath says you should. *Tell the truth, the whole truth and nothing but the truth.* I'll object to everything I can think of if he tries to bully you."

"He's going to rip me to shreds, isn't he?"

"I don't think so," Harte said. "I hope not."

She pushed her fingers through her hair and took a long breath. "I'm going to end up looking like an idiot and a liar to the judge and jury."

"No, you're not. You'll come across as earnest and sincere and heartbroken. Between us, we'll make sure the jury sees your honesty and integrity. I know you don't think so, but I'm a good prosecutor."

She studied him. "Oh, I know you're a good pros—"

Just then the wind picked up, flinging rain like gravel tapping against the big picture window in the living room.

Dani jumped. She drew up her shoulders and braced for more. Sure enough, lightning flashed as a sharp crack rent the air. She swallowed a shriek and vaulted up out of her chair.

"Hey," Harte said, rising. "It's okay."

"The storm's right on top of us. Do you think it's a tornado?" she asked tightly.

"Hopefully not. I'm thinking it will blow over soon. It should be moving north."

Dani nodded as she rubbed her arms. "I hope so."

He smiled that crooked smile. "Trust me," he said. "So, I'd like to keep going if you're up to it."

"I'm fine. Let me just get some water. The jambalaya made me thirsty."

"Yeah," he said, following her as she stepped over to the sink. "Me too."

As Dani reached for the tap, a huge burst of bright white light blinded her, a deafening explosion split the air and everything went black.

She screamed and flung herself toward Harte. Caught off guard, he stumbled backward when her weight hit him. "Dani—?" he started.

Her almost silent whimper cut him off. Her hands clutched at the front of his shirt. Instinctively he folded his arms around her. Her body trembled violently.

He breathed deeply and nearly groaned at the sweet melon scent of her hair. That delicious fragrance combined with the pressure of her body so tight against him ripped away at his normally rock-solid self-control. The soft firmness of her breasts, the slight bump of her hip bones, the feel of her warm breath on his neck, were as tantalizing as he'd known they'd be. He squeezed his eyes closed. He could learn to love the feel of her body pressed against his. He pulled her closer.

After a moment he turned his head and looked out the kitchen window. He couldn't see a thing. Not a pale porch bulb of a neighbor's house. Not a streetlight. Nothing.

"The lightning must have blown transformers all

over the area," he muttered. "There are no lights as far as I can see."

She nodded and more of the sweet scent of melon tickled his nose. He clenched his jaw as his body reacted. Damn it, he was on the edge of some very dangerous territory.

A vision of them together in bed taunted him. He struggled to banish it.

The only reason she threw herself into his arms was that she was terrified by the lightning and the darkness. She was seeking safety. If she had the slightest notion of his unprofessional thoughts, she'd be away from him like a shot and any trust he'd managed to build with her would be gone.

"Hey," he said, peering intently at her. He could barely make out her features in the darkness. "It's just a storm, that's all. You live in south Louisiana. It's not like you haven't been in a storm before, right?"

She stiffened and pushed away. "Right," she said shakily, then cleared her throat. "Sure. I'm fine. I've got a flashlight on my key ring. It's in my purse in the bedroom—"

"Hang on. I'm sure there are candles around here somewhere," he said. "Check the kitchen drawers." He turned and reached out for a drawer handle, found one and pulled, then searched inside. "Ow!" he exclaimed. "Be careful. I just pricked my finger on a knife."

"Is it bad?" she asked, sounding more like her old self.

"Nah." He stuck his fingertip in his mouth for a second, then continued searching. His hand closed around the distinctive shape of a lighter and next to it, the waxy tapered length of a candle. "Here we go," he said as he pulled them out.

He thumbed the lighter and lit the candle. The flickering light gleamed eerily as it reflected in her wide eyes. Her mouth was set in a tight line.

"Here," he said. "Take this. I'm sure there are more. I'll see if I can find something to hold them."

She held out her hand, her eyes glued to the flame.

Outside the thunder rumbled loudly and lightning flashed, lighting up the windows for a split second. She flinched and scrunched her shoulders. She was definitely afraid of storms. He felt a different emotion take hold of him. An urge to shelter her, protect her, hold on to her and reassure her that everything was going to be all right. It surprised him that he felt so protective toward her. She was one of the strongest, most determined women he'd ever met.

He touched her sleeve and felt her stiffen. "Storms really bother you, don't they?" he said gently.

She tried for a casual shrug, but her shoulders moved jerkily. "I'm fine."

"No, you're not. Tell me why storms scare you."

She sniffed in frustration. "Why storms scare me. Well, my father died in a tornado when I was seven. Maybe that's why."

"That's an awful thing for a little girl to go through."

She shrugged and the candlelight outlined her sad face in shadows. "I had this image of the tornado as a big whirling monster that ate everything in its path. When it storms like this, I can't wipe that image out of my mind."

Thunder rumbled again and she hugged herself.

"Don't worry," he whispered. "I'm right here."

Her gaze snapped to his, and her chin lifted. "I said I'm fine."

He considered what he'd been thinking about her seconds before and amended it. She was one of the strongest, most determined and most *stubborn* women he'd ever met.

He shrugged and turned his attention back to the drawer, looking for more candles. He found a few that had been burned down at least halfway. Those would be easier to set up. He lit one and began dripping wax on a saucer he took from the drain board.

"I have to get my purse," Dani said.

Harte nodded, still busy with the candle. He got it stuck to a saucer with wax, then started on a second one. "Now we've got several candles," he called. "This should last us until they get the power back on—"

A crash drowned out his words. His head snapped toward the window. Was that glass breaking? Or just the noise of the thunder?

"Harte!" Dani's panicked voice came from across the room.

"Dani?" he asked. He stuck a stubby candle and the lighter in his pocket as he hurried toward her.

"What was that—?"

He saw her and halted. Something wasn't right. The way her body was lit—the way shadows were flickering, almost dancing, as if tossed around by a fire.

A split second later, he knew what was wrong, but that was a split second too late. Dani had figured it out too. She was screaming and pointing behind him. He turned, already certain of what he would see.

In the middle of the hardwood floor, in front of the big picture window, surrounded by broken glass that glinted red and yellow and orange, was a bottle belching flames from its mouth. Flames that licked at the curtains and crawled across the floor.

Chapter Eight

As Harte watched the flames spread, another bottle sailed through the window and bounced and rolled. The first one was a Molotov cocktail. This one was a smoke bomb.

Yeoman's men. It had to be. Had they followed him from the courthouse through all the traffic? He should have been watching, should have been aware that he could be followed. His Jeep wasn't exactly the standard for the courthouse parking lot. They must have been waiting outside for the right moment.

He lunged toward Dani, grabbing the candle out of her hand and blowing it out. "They're trying to burn us out," he said. "I'm calling 911." He snatched his phone from his pocket, but he still had no service. He thumbed the three numbers anyway, but the phone just made a pinging noise and went back to the default screen. He dove toward the landline phone.

"How'd they find us?" Dani croaked.

"Get into your room. We'll go through the windows. My car's parked on that side." He grabbed the phone to dial 911, but the line was dead. The smoke from the bomb was filling the air as he ran toward the bedroom behind Dani. He'd break the tall windows and make a run for his car.

He hoped whoever was out there didn't have the house surrounded. The only thing that might save them was the darkness and the cover of the driving rain. Right now, though, lightning streaked the sky directly over their heads.

Just as he made it through the bedroom door, the biggest flash lit up the sky. It outlined two dark figures in the yard, moving toward the house. Dani was standing in front of her dresser, picking up something. He grabbed her by the hand. "There's someone out there. We've got to head for the kitchen."

She pulled away. "I need my purse!" she cried.

"It'll just get in your way!" he countered, but she grabbed it. As soon as she grasped the handle, he jerked her back out into the living room.

"Come on!" he croaked, coughing with every breath. The Molotov cocktail had burned itself out, but clouds of smoke still rose from the smoke bomb. Beside him, Dani was coughing and choking too.

He knew their only chance now was through the kitchen. He'd inspected the bed-and-breakfast thoroughly before he'd booked it. The manager had gladly turned the keys over to him and left to visit his grandkids in Baton Rouge. On the key ring was the master key to the house and another, smaller key. It went to a storeroom off the kitchen that opened onto an alley.

The manager had passed right by the door, but Harte had insisted on checking it out. The storeroom was small and dark, filled with cleaning supplies and boxes. It had an identical door on the other side of the room that led outside. On the outside, the door was finished just like the rest of the house. At a glance, it was impossible to tell it was a door.

All of that slid through his mind in the three long seconds it took for them to cross the living room. By the time they reached the small door, both of them were coughing constantly.

"Where are we going?" Dani asked, hanging back as he unlocked it.

"This goes to the alley. It's our only chance."

"What happened?" she cried. "How did they find us?"

"I don't know. I'll go first. Make sure they're not out there waiting for us." He unlocked the door to the outside and slipped through. With any luck, the men hadn't noticed the delivery door. They'd be guarding the front and back, poised to grab Dani when she was forced out by the smoke and flames. With a little luck, he just might get her out alive.

Harte pressed himself flat against the clapboard wall of the B & B. The rain was punishing, but the narrow overhang of the roof kept the worst off him. It didn't help with his vision, though. The veil of falling water obscured everything beyond a couple of feet. And if that weren't bad enough, it turned to steam as soon as it hit the hot asphalt. Everything was enveloped in swirling gray. Harte couldn't see anything or anyone. And he could barely hear through the rain's dull roar.

Dani touched his arm. "Harte?"

He held out his hand. "It's okay. Come on," he said as loudly as he could to be heard over the rain, "but be quiet."

She took his hand and stepped through the doorway, ducking her head and hunching her shoulders against the rain. She clutched her purse tightly. "Is it safe?" she asked.

Harte squinted at her, blinking against raindrops. "No, but it's the best chance we've—" He stopped. "Shh. Hold it," he whispered. Sure enough, he heard shouts coming from the front of the house.

He tugged on her hand. "Come on. We're going that way, up Race Street." He gestured in the opposite direction. "Can you keep up with me?" he asked.

"Yes," she said firmly.

He looked her up and down. She had on sneakers, thank goodness, and that huge purse was draped across her body like a messenger bag.

He plunged into the gray sheet of rain with Dani right behind him. He didn't want to run. They were too handicapped by the rain and the nearly impenetrable darkness. Of course the bad guys were handicapped by the downpour as well, but judging by the two men they'd seen and the shouts he'd heard, he feared that he and Dani were outnumbered by at least four to two.

All he could do was trust his instincts and try to get Dani to someplace safe.

He moved as fast as he could, tugging her with him until, out of nowhere, he stepped into a pothole. "Ahh!" he cried as his leg collapsed beneath him. He winced as pain shot up his leg from his ankle. He flexed it gently. To his relief, he could move it.

"Harte!" Dani knelt beside him as he tried to push himself to his feet. But when he put his weight on the ankle, a sharp throbbing stabbed him to the bone. *Damn it.* It was sprained. He knew from the first- and second-aid preparation courses he'd taken as a precaution for solo backpacking trips that he needed to wrap it as soon as he could. But right now he had no choice but to grit his teeth and bear it.

Dani touched his foot with her hand. "Is it broken?" she asked.

He grabbed her hand. "Get up. We've got to go." He knew the ankle was just sprained, not broken, but it hurt like a son of a bitch even so.

He pulled her to the edge of the alley. The rain was in his eyes, soaking his clothes and shoes. He tried his best to see whether there was a vehicle waiting for them on the far side, where the alley opened out onto Orange Street.

As far as he could tell, both the alley and the street beyond it were clear. He wiped his face on the drenched sleeve of his white shirt. It didn't help.

He headed across, pulling Dani with him, doing his best not to limp. A pair of glowing orbs was visible in the distance.

Headlights.

Dani saw it too. She squeezed his hand. "Harte! A car!"

"Hurry, before they see us." The vehicle was approaching much faster than it should have been, considering that the driver had to be barreling blindly through the rain.

They headed across the street and ducked under an overhang. Without the rain beating down on them, they both leaned gratefully against the side of the building, trying to catch their breaths.

Suddenly, the whole street lit up as another flash of lightning ripped through the sky, followed by a deafening roar. The rain, which was already a downpour, now fell in sheets.

"Harte—" Dani cried.

He blinked as he desperately tried to see through the beating rain. It was dangerous and stupid to stumble blindly around without knowing where they were headed.

He'd studied the streets near the B & B, but the combination of the rain and the darkness was doubly disorienting, and there was no hope of reading a street sign from more than a few inches away.

"Harte!" She tugged on his shirtsleeve and stood on tiptoe to get close to his ear. "Look. The headlights aren't moving."

He focused on the pallid, blurry spots of the headlights. They were still. He blinked and looked again. The vehicle was still moving, but more slowly. Then he noticed dark shadows in front of it, heading in their direction. But he couldn't tell how many. Two? Three?

"It's them!" Dani cried.

Harte tightened his hand around her wrist and jerked her with him as he ran unevenly, gritting his teeth against the pain in his ankle.

He spotted a darker rectangle in the midst of the gray. The entrance to the alley? God, he hoped so. If he was wrong, they'd be sitting ducks. He sped up, tightening his grip on Dani's wrist.

But moving forward through the rain was like pushing through a maze of heavy drapes while fording a stream, because the water rushing around their feet was at least three inches deep, making the roads slippery. And the pain in his ankle wasn't helping. He stumbled and his fingers slipped off Dani's wrist.

That quickly, she was gone.

Dani lost her footing when her hand slid out of Harte's grip. Her knee hit the wet pavement, hard. With a small cry she tried to regain her footing. But the road was too slippery; the rain pressed on her shoulders like a heavy hand and she was quickly losing strength from fighting it.

Where was Harte? She squinted through the rain and held her breath, listening. The drumming roar of the rain was confusing and disorienting. It was impossible to tell where any sound came from.

Straining, she thought she heard Harte's voice calling her name. But she couldn't tell for sure. Heading in what she hoped was the right direction, she was tempted to call out, but what if it wasn't him? Was she heading toward Harte or was she about to plow right into her pursuers?

She wiped her face on her sleeve, for all the good it did, and pushed her heavy, soaked hair back.

At that instant, the roar in her ears changed in pitch. She squinted, as if that would help her see. A dark rumble rose from beneath the rain's din. The sound was not thunder, but mechanical, rhythmic. Like a car engine.

Frightened by the closeness of the sound, she felt the hairs on the nape of her neck prickling. She blinked, trying to see. Why didn't Harte call out again? She couldn't tell which way to run. The rumble grew louder, seeming to surround her.

Lightning flashed. She swallowed a shriek and barely

stopped herself from diving to the ground, but from what little she could see around her, she was in the middle of a street, completely exposed. Thunder cracked and roared. She moaned in fear and frustration as she trudged on.

Pushing against the rising, punishing wind, she squinted, looking for anything she could use for shelter. A dark building loomed just ahead. Her pulse jumped in excitement.

She trudged toward it, hoping to slip into an alley or a corner where the car couldn't go, praying that she could find Harte.

As she wiped rain off her nose, she thought she heard his voice again. But then a car door slammed right behind her. That sound was unmistakable—and way too close. Terror crawled up her spine and twisted her insides. She had to run. Lowering her head, she pressed forward, her legs beginning to ache with the effort of pushing against the wind and rain. She prayed she was going in the right direction.

The rain, the lightning and her imagination were distorting everything—what she saw, what she heard. She squinted against the gray rain. She could no longer see the building she'd been headed for.

Her toe struck something and sent her sprawling. Her hands took the brunt of the fall, sliding and scraping across rough wet concrete, and her shin banged painfully against a hard edge. She bit her cheek to keep from crying out.

She'd tripped over a curb. Behind her, heavy footsteps reverberated across the ground. She didn't dare turn around to see, but she knew from the sound that they were almost on top of her. With a great deal of effort, she managed to get her feet under her and gain some traction. Just as she straightened, a bright flash of lightning lit the street. This time she couldn't resist. She turned to look.

A large dark form barreled toward her, too big and broad to be Harte. In the same second, she heard Harte's voice clearly.

"Dani!"

But it was impossible to pinpoint where it had come from. Directly in front of her? Ahead and to the left? She heard the man chasing her and wondered if she had time to dig her gun out of her purse. But he was too close. So close she could see color beginning to seep through the gray. The dark blob turned to a dull tan, and as he lumbered toward her she realized that it was a raincoat with the collar turned up. Although she'd already figured out that it wasn't Harte, still her throat seized, cutting off her breath.

She tried to run and almost fell again when she put her weight on her knee. "Harte! Here! They're after me!" she screamed. She didn't care if the man in the raincoat heard her. He was so close that she imagined she could hear his heaving breaths over the downpour. Letting Harte know her location was her only chance.

"Harte!" she shouted again, but her voice was gobbled up by thunder. Then a strong hand grabbed the back of her shirt and jerked her off her feet.

Chapter Nine

Harte heard Dani's terrified scream, cut off by thunder, but he couldn't tell where she was. He'd been retracing his steps ever since he lost hold of her hand. She should have been only a few feet behind him, if she'd stayed put. She must have gotten turned around and been moving away from him all this time.

He heard another short cry. Had they found her? He pushed forward, praying that the shriek he'd heard had just been her startled reaction to the thunder and lightning.

Then he saw it. A big black shadow, rising out of the mist. The car. He slowed down, cautiously keeping an eye on it. Then he detected another difference in the constant gray of rain and wind. He wiped his face, then blinked. He saw movement. Something large and brown and vaguely human shaped. It had to be one of Yeoman's men.

Did he have Dani? Harte couldn't tell. He moved slowly and steadily toward the man, hoping not to attract notice. But then he caught a splash of red—her shirt. Adrenaline burned through him like flaming jet fuel.

The man did have her. He was dragging her toward the car.

Harte had only one chance and it was a slim one. Balancing himself on his right foot, he dove, aiming at the man's knees. He hit what felt like solid rock. The impact rattled his teeth and echoed in his head, but the man fell like a dead tree, slamming into the pavement.

Harte ducked and rolled out of his way. He came to rest not ten inches from the front fender of the car. It was smashed and the headlights were broken—damaged, no doubt, from ramming Dani's front porch. Glancing over his shoulder, Harte saw the big man flip over onto his stomach. He waved his arms and legs like a turtle, trying to get his hands underneath him. Too soon, the man managed to get to his hands and knees. He shook his massive head and made a noise that echoed through the pounding rain like a lion's roar. Then he propelled himself forward.

Harte scrambled to his feet. The goon had brute strength going for him, but he was about as graceful as a bull elephant. Harte heard his sawing breaths coming closer and closer.

Harte waited until the last possible second, hoping that the other man was as disoriented by the rain as he was, before diving out of the way. Luckily, the brute had built up enough momentum that he couldn't stop. He obviously counted on Harte to break his fall. He hit the ground, hard.

Harte regained his balance and looked inside the attacker's car. It was empty. Dani wasn't there. Hot fear pulsed through him. Where was she? Did one of the other men have her?

And where were the other three men?

Were they on foot, sneaking around to ambush him,

or had they taken Dani somewhere? As he turned, he caught a glimpse of a dark figure rising from behind a trash receptacle. Another man rose right beside him. Before he could react, both men lifted their arms and he heard the unmistakable crack of gunfire muffled by the rain. Before the shots faded, he heard Dani scream behind him.

"Dani!" he yelled, whirling and spotting a splash of red through the gray curtain of rain. It was Dani! She was on the ground, several feet away from the car. His gut clenched. Had she been hit?

He sprang toward her, wrapping his fingers around her upper arm and yanking her upright, quickly scanning her clothes for blood. He didn't see any. "Are you hit?" he yelled.

"No!" She shook her head. "Are you?"

Behind them, he heard car doors opening and closing. He tried to count, but the sounds were too muffled by the storm. Maybe two, maybe three. The men had gotten back into the car.

"They're in the car. Run!" he shouted before pumping his legs, pulling her with him. Behind them, more gunshots rang out and he heard men shouting. He pulled her behind a parked van.

"Get that shirt off!" he cried.

"What? My shirt?"

He turned her around and grabbed the collar, jerking it over her head. "It's too bright."

After tossing it over a nearby parking meter, Harte pointed toward a narrow alleyway in front of them and yelled in her ear, "Through there!" Grabbing her arm, he tightened his grip. He wasn't going to lose her again.

Dani half ran, half stumbled alongside Harte. The only thing that kept her from collapsing onto the drenched pavement was the painful grasp of his hand on her arm—the same arm the thug had bruised when he'd grabbed her.

She could hear the pop-pop-pop of gunfire behind them, and her shoulders tightened reflexively. Then she heard the deep revving of a car engine. Harte had stunned her attacker enough to make him let go of her, but they were in their car now, and it would be no time until they caught up with them again. She could barely catch her breath in the rain, and in only her white tank top, the chill had long since seeped under her skin. She gritted her teeth and concentrated on staying on her feet. As Harte led her into the dark recesses of the alley, she glanced around in trepidation. She hoped he knew where he was going.

The overhanging roofs gave a bit of protection from the rain. Once they were safely underneath, Harte slowed to a walk, then to a stop.

Dani wiped her face and squeezed water out of her hair as she gulped in huge lungfuls of air. All at once, a massive shudder shook her, a delayed reaction to the brutish thug's hand on her. Between that and the cold, she couldn't stop shaking.

"Harte, are you shot?" she panted. She didn't see any blood, but he hadn't answered her when she'd asked before.

Beside her, Harte leaned against the building's wall. He shook his head, breathing hard. After a few seconds, he straightened and looked toward the entrance of the alley, listening. "Come on," he said. "We've got to keep going."

"Where?" she asked as he grabbed her hand.

A bit of brightness behind them rose through the gray like a hazy sunrise. "It's the car," he said. "Move!"

But as he moved into the alley, he saw that it was a dead end. A high wooden fence stretched between the two buildings. They were trapped. Twisting back, Harte could see the headlights. They'd blocked the entrance of the alley. He saw two men climbing out, then a third.

Without waiting to see if a fourth man got out, Harte pushed Dani behind him so his body would shield her as he desperately searched for an escape. Even if they could climb the fence, they'd be sitting ducks. Then he saw a door set into a side wall. "This way," he said. "Stay behind me."

He rattled the doorknob, then stepped back and rammed the door with his shoulder. Nothing happened. He took two steps back, prepared to ram the door again, but Dani grabbed his arm.

"Get out of the way! I've got this!" Dani cried. She grabbed the lock-pick set from her purse and unsnapped the cover. Her hands were soaking wet, just like the rest of her, and shaking with cold and fear, but she managed to pick up the right tool. She shouldered her way in front of Harte, bent over the doorknob and after a shaky false start, got the pick inserted into the lock.

Harte grabbed her upper arm. "Dani, what are you doing? They're coming. Get behind me."

Gritting her teeth, she worked the pick.

"Dani!"

"Wait," she snapped as the tumblers slid. "The door's

open. Let's go." She opened the door and grabbed his arm, pulling him inside. She kept her grip on the knob as Harte stumbled in behind her, then slammed the door shut and turned the dead bolt. They were inside and, at least for the moment, safe from the faceless men pursuing them. Collapsing back against Harte, her eyes closed, she gasped for breath. She'd done it. She'd picked the lock. She couldn't count the number of times she'd picked all the locks in her granddad's house, learning the feel of the tools and the faint differences between tumblers sliding apart and slipping back together. But she'd never dreamed she'd actually use her knowledge in a life-and-death situation for real.

Her pulse was racing so fast that it echoed in her ears. Harte wrapped his arms around her shoulders from behind, pulling her closer against him. His chest rose and fell against her back. His breath was cool across her wet forehead. With a sigh, she let herself relax against his long, lean body. Through their wet clothes, she felt the heat of his body envelop her. A shudder, equal parts cold, fear and desire, shook her.

"Dani?" he whispered.

She went still. Did he want her to move? She hoped not, because she didn't want to leave the heat of his body. She was soaked, and while April in New Orleans could hardly be called cold, even in the rain, she felt chilled to the bone.

As she waited to see what he was going to say, she concentrated on the feel of him pressed against her. Warmth wasn't all she needed from him now. She greedily soaked up the feelings of safety, comfort and a deep, rich yearning she'd never felt before.

He was silent and still for a long moment. His breath had calmed, and she could feel his heart beating fast but steadily against her back. Or at least she imagined she could.

He lowered his head and whispered in her ear, "How the hell did you do that?" She felt his lips graze the sensitive skin of her ear, and her insides quivered with longing. It took her a moment to figure out what he was talking about.

"Oh, the lock," she muttered; then deliberately, she turned her head so that her mouth was close to his. "I picked it," she whispered.

He made a small noise like a gasp as her mouth brushed his. "You what?"

"Picked the lock. Granddad gave me his lock-pick kit when I was ten. He said, 'You never know when you might need to get through a door.'"

She felt his chest rumble with laughter. "That's illegal."

"So sue me," she said lightly, then turned in his arms, rose on her tiptoes and kissed him. It was a tentative brushing of lips against lips, but it sent desire arrowing through her, all the way down to her toes.

Harte lifted his head slightly, and Dani moved with him, straining upward, keeping her mouth against his. For a moment that seemed suspended outside of time, he didn't move, and then she felt him relent. It was a subtle relaxing of his tense muscles, a tiny dip of his head as he took the kiss to the next level. She felt his tongue touch her mouth, felt his arm slide from her shoulders down her back to pull her even closer...

She lifted her head to meet his deeper kiss, just as

an odd sound broke through the steady drumbeat of the rain.

Harte stiffened—he'd heard it too.

Her heart skipped a beat. "Do I hear shouting?" she breathed.

He nodded. "Right outside the door," Harte whispered as the noise suddenly stopped. He straightened slowly, his hand still around her waist. "Move away—without a sound."

She opened her eyes for the first time and met a solid wall of darkness. She held out her hands in front of her, trying to keep her balance. Total darkness was so disorienting. She felt as though a single misstep would send her tumbling into a bottomless pit. She wanted to close her eyes again. She wanted to be back in Harte's arms.

Finally, slowly, she became aware of a faint lessening of the total dark. She searched, making herself dizzy, until she found its source—small windows set high in the walls of the warehouse. At last, she had something she could look at to maintain her balance. She took one cautious step, then another. She braced herself, not wanting to crash into something.

By her fourth step, she'd nearly convinced herself that she could see vague shadows in the darkness. Whether they were real or figments of her imagination, being able to focus on something made her feel better.

Then her fingers touched something. She gasped. "There's something here," she whispered to Harte.

"Keep going, slowly," he whispered back. "What does it feel like?"

"Paper?" she said, but that wasn't quite right. It was too hard. "No. Plastic?" she guessed.

She started to take another step, but Harte laid a hand on her shoulder from behind.

"Wait," he said, stopping.

"What is it?"

"Shh."

She held her breath, but didn't hear anything. "You heard them, didn't you?" she whispered.

She felt Harte shake his head. "Not yet. But they will be here soon," he said grimly.

"Maybe they doubled back to look at the building. We don't know how many doors there are." She paused. "Or if they're all locked."

Suddenly, the door they'd come through rattled. The men were trying to force it open. Then a ferocious pounding filled the air. They were kicking the metal door.

"Keep going," he said. "We need to get away from there, and fast. I need to see how many other entrances there are."

His words were cut off by a sharp, ricocheting sound. "They're trying to shoot the lock. They gave up on forcing the metal door open."

"The lock's a Schlage," Dani said. "It'll take them forever to break it by shooting at it."

"It's a what?"

"A Schlage. The strongest and most reliable padlock in the world. Granddad had Schlage locks on every door. When you've tried to pick one, you develop a healthy respect for them."

Several rounds fired within a few seconds. Each

one ricocheted just like the first. Then they heard more shouting.

"Maybe one of them caught a ricochet," she said hopefully.

"Maybe it's the boss, telling them to surround the building," Harte replied.

"Surround?" she said in surprise. "How many men do you think are out there? I only saw three."

"I think there are four, unless there's another vehicle. I don't think so, though. I can't believe these guys can still maneuver that car out there, with all the wind and rain. Come on. We need to find a place to hide."

"Why can't we just wait here until they give up and then sneak back out this door?"

"If I were the boss, I'd find the freight door and try to ram it with the car." He took her hand and started forward, into the blackness.

As soon as she put out her hand, it bumped a solid, rounded surface in front of her. "Oh, wait. I've got a flashlight," Dani said, fishing in her purse. "I forgot about it."

She felt him shrug. Then he said, "You've got a lot of stuff in that purse, don't you?"

She couldn't help chuckling. "You have no idea."

"What does that mean?" he asked.

She pulled the flashlight out and turned it on. The narrow beam shone on a massive, gaping red-and-blue mouth lined with dozens of sharp white teeth. It loomed over her, poised to rip her apart. She stared into the gaping maw, a shriek ripping its way past her tight throat.

After a moment of paralyzing fear, she whirled and grasped at Harte's shirt as she tried to suck air into lungs that felt collapsed with terror. She held on to him with all her might.

Harte pulled her close and took the flashlight from her numb fingers. A noise like laughter rumbled up from his chest. *Laughter?* Carefully, she turned her head enough to peek back at the thing that had nearly attacked her.

Harte shone the flashlight's beam over the monster's dreadful eyes, gleaming white teeth and garish slashes of color. Her knee-jerk reaction was to bury her face in the hollow of his shoulder. But there was something familiar about the garish face. Her cheeks began to warm as she figured out what she was looking at.

Harte laughed out loud. "I've heard about these, but I've never seen one," he said, chuckling. "We're in a warehouse used to store Mardi Gras floats."

She unclenched her fists from his shirt and turned around. Slowly, with Harte shining the flashlight around, the nightmarish bloody beasts morphed into the familiar fiberglass, crepe paper and feather decorations she'd seen in every Mardi Gras parade.

The awful mouth with its razor-sharp teeth that had threatened to devour her belonged to a colorful Chinese dragon head mounted on the front end of a brightly painted double-decker float dripping with gold, purple and green Mardi Gras beads.

Next to the dragon was a gigantic leprechaun face topped with a kelly-green hat. She remembered seeing both floats in last year's parade.

Similar garish and vaguely disturbing shapes stretched beyond them until they melted into the darkness. Even though she knew what they were now, the back of her throat still fluttered with fading terror and she couldn't stop shivering. "This can't be Mardi Gras World?"

He shook his head, still chuckling. "No. You've seen Mardi Gras World, right? It's a museum. This is just a storage warehouse."

"Stop laughing," she snapped. "I was scared."

"Sorry," he responded, but the amused tone was still there. "Shh," he said. "Listen."

She did. The shooting and banging had stopped. "I don't hear anything."

"I think they've abandoned that door," he said.

"You think they're looking for the freight door?"

"It's what I would do. If I only had four men, I'd leave one at the door we came in and the rest of us would look for the best way to break in…" As he talked, he fished his phone from his pocket and flipped it open. "I've still got nothing." He pressed a couple of buttons. "Can't call out or send a message."

"The storm must have knocked out a bunch of cell towers."

Harte nodded. "If we can't call for help, they can't either. Let's go," he said. "I want to see where the freight door is—and how many other doors there are. Then we can plan how we're going to get out of here." Glancing around, he continued. "If we're careful, we can use the floats like a maze. There must be thirty in here, maybe forty."

"That's thirty or forty too many for me. They're creepy."

"Come on," he said, leading the way into the darkness lit only by the flashlight's narrow beam. She followed his winding trail through the dozens of floats, giving the huge fiberglass monster heads as wide a berth as she could while still keeping up with him.

He stopped abruptly and she almost ran into him.

"Here's the freight door. It looks pretty sturdy and it's on the opposite side of the building from the door we came in." He glanced around. "They're going to use their car to break it in, I'll guarantee you. Come on. Let's circle around this side of the building." He gestured. "Stay away from both the freight door and the door you opened."

They made their way diagonally away from the freight door. When they reached the wall, Harte slid along it, feeling for a door. Dani stayed behind him.

"Here," he said finally. "If I haven't totally lost my bearings, I think this door is just about halfway between the freight door and the one we came in and on the opposite wall." He caught her hand and drew it toward him. "Feel the lock. Is it like the one you picked?"

"It feels like a Schlage. It's got a turn bolt on the inside, just like that one. All we should have to do is turn the latch and open the door."

"Great," he said.

"Do you want me to open it now?"

"Hang on a minute and listen."

Dani heard pounding and shouting and an occasional gunshot. "Won't the police hear the gunshots?"

"In a storm like this? I'm guessing the only reason we can hear them is something about steel and echoes. That's not my area of expertise. But outside, in the rain and the thunder? I doubt that noise they're making will carry for twenty-five feet."

"How long is it going to take them to break in?"

She felt his shoulders move in a shrug, and a small thrill slid through her. Now that she'd kissed him, she was reacting to his every slightest move. He was tall and graceful and rock-hard. His skin was like silk over steel. Everything about him radiated warmth and safety and a sexuality that drew her to him like a moth to a flame.

She shivered. "Will you hold me for a minute?" she asked.

For a brief, heart-stopping moment, he hesitated. Then he slid his arm around her shoulders. His wet shirt against her thinly covered breasts caused goose bumps to rise on her skin. She felt a fine trembling in his muscles.

Was he chilled in his wet clothes, or was he as affected by their closeness as she was? She hoped he was. At that instant, he bent his head and laid his cheek against hers. With a sigh, she lifted her chin slightly, so that her lips brushed his skin.

"How's your ankle?" she whispered, looking up at him. His face was barely visible in the almost pitch-black. Light from the small windows glittered in his deep brown eyes. His breath drifted across her sensitized lips, making them tremble with the need to feel his mouth, his body, pressing against her.

"Harte?" she said, hearing the question in her voice and wondering if he would hear it and understand it. She felt odd, almost weightless, as if she were floating. She ached with wanting him, and that frightened her. Because he wasn't interested in her at all, except as his witness. The thoughts flitted through her head in the space of a single breath.

"What is it?" he answered, his voice unsteady.

A niggling question at the edge of her brain almost brought her up short. What was she doing? Harte Delancey was the last person she should be having sexy fantasies about. Sure, she'd been fascinated by him and his good looks from the first moment she'd faced him across the courtroom, but his superior attitude had been a turnoff. She'd decided back then that she was only interested in him because of his notorious legacy and their grandfathers' feud. That was still the only reason for her interest, right? That and the fact that he was breathtakingly handsome.

Enveloped in his arms, with the citrusy scent of his shampoo and the warmth radiating from his body, she knew she was kidding herself. She couldn't deny how much she desired him. He was so much more than arrogance and a pretty face. He was strength and confidence and compassion. And she needed all three.

Despite the pounding rain and the men trying to kill her, all she wanted to do was to stay here, wrapped in Harte's gentle yet sensual caress. Longing sent a shiver through her.

He pressed his lips to the corner of her mouth. "Are you cold?" he whispered, his breath tickling her skin.

"No," she whispered on a sigh. Heat flowed like lava through her entire body. Out to her fingertips and toes and back, swirling through her to her core. She bit her cheek to keep from moaning with pleasure.

He lifted his head slightly and even in the dim light she could see that his firm, wide mouth had softened. Was he really about to kiss her right here in the middle of running from people who were trying to kill them?

She should say something. Should stop this. Because all they were doing was seeking comfort in a dangerous situation. The men outside were a danger to her, but so was Harte. And right now she wasn't sure who frightened her most.

By the time she'd decided that it would not be in her best interest to kiss him, his lips were trailing across hers.

She reacted with a tiny gasp and he took the opportunity of her parted lips to kiss her—really kiss her. Then he dipped his head a little more and tasted her mouth. His tongue urged her lips apart and he deepened the kiss.

Her reaction was so immediate, so intense. It scared her. She had to regain control. Didn't she? Because if she didn't, she was going to sink into him, take his kisses and give them back. She was going to beg him to make love to her.

Harte shifted and her taut, sensitized nipples pressed into his flesh. Electricity sang along her nerve endings, centering in the most sensitive part of her. And that quickly, the desire spread through every inch of her body. The tips of her fingers and toes, the hairs on her neck, the skin on the insides of her wrists—all were now erogenous zones, waiting for his touch to ignite their fire.

"Harte—?" Her breath caught.

He froze. "Listen."

She held her breath, but couldn't hear anything except the rain and the quick, excited beating of her heart. After a couple of seconds she heard it. A faraway whining sound, like a car engine revving, came from the far end of the warehouse. "Is that—?" she started.

"They're going to ram the freight door with their car."

The engine noise grew louder and tires screeched; then the air was split by a deafening crash. Harte was still as a cat waiting for its prey. Another crash, much louder than the first, echoed through the warehouse.

"It's working," he said, setting her away from him. "The car's ripping a hole in the freight door."

Just then a third crash, louder and longer than the other two, echoed through the warehouse. As the squeal of tortured metal faded, the sound of voices became evident, echoing clearly off the metal walls.

"Son of a— What the hell is all this?"

"Hey, look! Mardi Gras floats!"

"Must be fifty of 'em—"

"It'll take hours to search all—"

"Just torch the whole—"

"Hang on! That ain't what Mr.—"

"Smoke 'em out, or let 'em burn up."

Dani's hand tightened on his arm. "They're going to burn the warehouse down," she whispered anxiously.

Harte pressed a finger against her lips. The men were still talking.

"How're we—?"

"Get over here and listen—"

Then the voices died down.

"We've got to get out of here," Harte said. "These floats will go up like dry kindling, and fiberglass fumes are toxic." When he stood, the dim light angled harshly off the rigid line of his jaw.

"Let's go. Are you sure all we have to do is turn the bolt on the door?"

"I think so. It looks just like the other one," she responded.

On the other side of the warehouse, the voices rose again and a small orange glow pierced the darkness.

"Wow! They sure burn fast—"

"Get outta the way!"

"Careful or—"

The glow steadily got brighter. Just as Harte had thought, the floats were catching fire with incredible speed. Within seconds, the glow had quadrupled in size and he could see smoke and smell the harsh fumes.

Chapter Ten

Harte moved toward the door with Dani right behind him. On the other side of the building, a roaring whoosh of air indicated more floats going up in flames. The acrid fumes grew worse. Dani coughed, and the sound echoed off the walls.

"Listen!"

Dani clapped her hand over her mouth.

"You!" a loud, gruff voice said. "Go around. They'll be smoked out in no time. Find the doors! Don't let them get away."

Harte reached the door and flipped the lock. He stopped, trying to get his bearings. If they were on the opposite side of the warehouse from the door they'd come in, then which way should they go? His best guess was to the right.

"Harte?" Dani sounded nervous.

"You stay behind me and follow me. I'm turning right. But keep up. I may have to change direction. If there's someone outside the door waiting for us, you stay inside until I can take care of him. Understand?"

She looked as though she wanted to say something, but she didn't. She nodded and covered her mouth again, coughing as quietly as she could.

He turned the bolt and pushed on the door, opening it a crack and checking to be sure the coast was clear. The only thing he saw through the silvery haze of rain was the dark, wet alley. Carefully, he pushed the door wider and stuck his head out. Nothing.

He slipped through the door with Dani right behind him. The alley was somewhat protected from the storm, but he heard the wind. It roared as it whipped around corners and flung rain at awnings, street signs and shutters in all directions. Paper and trash swirled and flapped against curbs and walls.

"Stay right behind me," he told her. They hugged the wall of the warehouse until they reached the street. He stopped Dani with a hand, then pressed himself against the building. He peeked out, trying to see both ends of the street without exposing himself.

So far they were in the clear. "Looks like we beat them here. But they're going to be right behind us," he said, pointing to the right. "This way."

Dani started to move, but Harte stopped her. He leaned close to her ear. "The wind is worse than it was," he said. "Hook your fingers into my belt. If you lose your grip, *do not move*. I'll find you."

She nodded and he felt her fingers slide beneath the waistband of his pants. He wrapped an arm around her and hooked a finger through one of the belt loops of her jeans. "Okay," he said. "Ready."

When they emerged from the alley and onto the street, the wind nearly knocked Dani's feet out from under her, but she held on to Harte's belt. He braced himself, tightened his grip on her belt loop and turned as directly into the wind as he could. He had learned on a winter hike in the Rockies that when his back was to the wind it was more difficult to maintain balance and control.

Once they were clear of the alley, the wind, rain and thunder quickly drowned out any other sound. Harte was acutely aware that a vehicle could be upon them before they could hear its engine. He trudged on, favoring his strained ankle and trying to ignore the prickling at the back of his neck. He wanted to put as much distance as possible between them and the men who were chasing them.

He was pretty sure the warehouse was west of the bed-and-breakfast. At least that was the direction he'd started out. He had a good sense of direction, but the combination of the darkness, the wind and the rain were playing havoc with his usual calm assurance.

He knew he was disoriented by the rain, but his best guess was that the wind was coming from the south, since that had been the projected path of the storm. That meant if they kept facing into it, they'd be moving farther away from the bed-and-breakfast.

The pelting of the rain on his face and hands stung like blackberry briars, making it hard to keep his eyes open. Dani was having the same problem; plus, with her eyes closed, the wind was pummeling her, causing her to stumble.

Harte pulled her close to his side. He wiped his face with the soaked cuff of his shirt, not that it did much good. Lowering his head, he continued on.

Then everything stopped. Harte had been leaning so far into the wind that he almost toppled forward. He stood still, looking around and listening. Amazingly the wind had suddenly calmed, the rain had stopped and the thunder had quieted. The silence was eerie, intense, as if the storm were holding its breath.

"What happened?" Dani asked.

"It's the eye of the storm," he replied, and started walking again, urging her along with him. "We need to take advantage of it. Come on!"

Without the wind and rain fighting them, it was much easier to walk. Harte blinked and used his drenched shirt cuff again to wipe his face. Looking around, he saw that most of the buildings were old, with fading paint and unreadable signs. Several appeared abandoned. He didn't recognize anything. He looked up and down the street. He needed to find a corner. If he could just get to a street sign, he'd know where he was, he was sure.

"Let's go this way," he said to Dani, pointing to the left. They'd only gone a few steps when she grabbed his arm.

"Listen," she hissed.

Harte stopped. At first he didn't hear anything. He held his breath.

"Is that voices—?" Dani said, her tone rising in a question.

"Yeah. Hurry!" He'd glanced at the buildings, hoping he'd recognize the street. Now he looked at them again, assessing which one would be best for them to hide in.

It was impossible to tell what most of the buildings were. Office buildings, probably. Harte grimaced. They'd be dry, but what could they offer other than shelter? He'd passed four seemingly identical facades before, tucked into the corner of one of the buildings, he saw a sign for a diner. That could be a little better. The diner would have food—and knives.

Then, in the distance, obscured by the damp haze that still hung in the air, he saw an old, distinctively shaped sign, rocking lazily back and forth on the chains that held it suspended above a set of glass doors.

He blinked, then squinted. It was an Rx sign. A drugstore. His heart skipped a beat. Considering the predicament they were in, hiding out in a drugstore would be like taking shelter in Santa's workshop. If they could get inside, they might be able to find more flashlights. Maybe even some dry clothes.

"Drugstore," he said to Dani, pointing toward it as he picked up his pace.

Then, as suddenly as the storm had quieted, it started up again. The sky dumped rain as if by giant bucketfuls. The wind blew it into their faces like tiny, stinging darts. Thunder rumbled in the distance. Then a blinding flash of lightning lit everything, and Harte read the faded words on the sign. Delaughter's Drugs and Sundries.

He bent his head toward Dani's ear. "When we step onto the street, the wind's going to blow us sideways. Walk steadily and deliberately. Be careful. The water looks like it's about four inches. It's flowing fast. If the wind doesn't knock you off your feet, the water will." He wrapped an arm around her waist. "Ready?"

She nodded. They stepped into the street. Dani faltered, but caught herself with Harte's help. When they were about halfway across, a harsh scraping noise rose above the roar of the rain and wind. Harte turned. A metal street sign, battered into a twisted mess by the punishing gusts of wind, was tumbling down the street, directly at them.

Harte threw himself to the pavement with Dani in his arms. "Hold your breath!" he yelled in her ear as he ducked his head and covered her head with his hands.

He cringed, praying the sharp-edged runaway sign wouldn't hit them. A rush of air on the nape of his neck and a discordant twang told him the sign passed way too close over them. A few inches lower and its jagged edges would have sliced right through them. He looked up in time to see one sharp edge of the piece of metal cut a fallen tree branch in half and not even slow down.

It took him a couple of seconds to calm his labored breathing.

Dani still lay beneath him, not moving.

"Dani?" he said, loosening his hold on her.

She took a gasping breath. He rolled off her and helped her up. Then they ran toward the drugstore.

Without even checking his stride, Harte used his forward momentum to kick at the glass entry door until it cracked. He half fell against the door when his ankle gave way, but he caught himself. Gritting his teeth, he kicked again and again, until the glass in the lower half of the door shattered. He reached in and unlatched the door from the inside. He pushed it open and pulled her inside, then closed it and latched it, for whatever good it would do, now that the bottom half was gone.

"Stay down," he ordered Dani as he quickly assessed the interior layout of the store. Directly in front of them was the cashier's cage, which was encased in a thick glass that Harte figured was bulletproof. Perfect. He guided Dani around behind the cage and they collapsed onto the floor with their backs against the wall, their shoulders touching. Harte felt Dani shivering.

"How're you doing?" he asked.

She nodded as she pushed wet hair out of her eyes. "I'm okay," she said, flinging water off her hands. "I used to think that walking in the rain was fun." He took a good look at her face. She was pale, but she seemed to be fine. He breathed a sigh of relief. They'd made it.

"Stay here. I'm going to check the street." He got up, wiping water off his face and head. Now that he had Dani in a safe place, he wanted to make sure they hadn't been followed. He didn't think so, but in truth, it had been impossible to see well enough to be sure.

He positioned himself with his back in the corner between the front window and the wall and surveyed the street. Everywhere they'd been, once the storm started, the streets had been deserted. Not even a dog or a cat. New Orleans people and animals knew better than to fight a storm.

The street was flowing with water, and the rain was still coming down. The sky above the tops of the buildings seemed to be almost constantly lit with flashes of lightning. This was the worst kind of spring storm, and like many of them, it was caught right over the Port of New Orleans. Harte hadn't seen or heard any tornadoes, but he knew this kind of storm could spawn them— sometimes by the dozen. They'd been lucky so far.

After he'd done his best to scan every corner and alley and scrutinize every shadow, he headed back behind the cashier's counter and sat down beside Dani.

"There doesn't seem to be even a rat moving out there. We should be okay here for a while," he told her, brushing water off his face again, then leaned his head back against the wall. When he closed his eyes, he could see the metal sign, tumbling toward them. That had been a close call. Too close. He didn't have to work hard to conjure up a vision of that piece of twisted steel slicing through them. He shuddered. At least they were finally safe. For now.

DANI COULDN'T REMEMBER ever being so tired or scared in her life. Not even on the night her grandfather was murdered. She'd been scared in the B & B when the lights had gone out. And she'd been afraid when the men had started burning the warehouse floats. But neither of those things had compared with the terror that had overwhelmed her when Harte had suddenly grabbed her and dove to the ground with her in tow. She'd had no idea what was happening. She'd heard the metallic whistling of something passing over their heads. At first she'd thought the sound was bullets, whistling close by her ears, but it droned on for too long. Then she'd heard a harsh screech in front of them. The whole while, she'd scrunched her shoulders, expecting some kind of blow at any second. When Harte rolled off her, and she'd raised her head, she'd caught a fleeting glimpse of a bent, jagged-edged sign as it disappeared into the gray distance.

She shuddered now, recalling the sight. "That sign. It b-barely missed us," she muttered, shuddering.

Harte didn't answer.

"You saved my life—again."

Drops of water from her hair dripped down the back of her neck. She didn't want to move, but the chilly drops were tickling her back. She gathered her hair in her hands and squeezed it, shivering as the water ran in rivulets down her neck and between her breasts.

Her eyes burned and her throat clogged. She felt tears welling. She'd been a hairbreadth away from death three times within a week. Harte shifted, then turned on the flashlight. The beam was weak and pale.

"Oh no, the battery's nearly dead," Dani said.

Harte turned his gaze to hers. His eyes twinkled in the pallid light. "But we're in a drugstore."

She got it immediately. "And drugstores sell batteries," she said, her mouth turning up in a smile.

"Right." He stood, shining the flashlight's beam around.

"They're usually close to the register, aren't they?"

"Yep. Here we go." He walked out of her sight and after a moment she heard paper tearing. When he came back and sat down, he handed the mini-flashlight to her. Then he tore more cardboard.

"What's that?" she asked, shining the beam on what he held.

"A bigger flashlight." He finished inserting the batteries, then turned it on.

Dani shielded her eyes. "Ow, too much. We've been in the dark too long."

"Watch this." He clicked a button and the intense brightness went away and a softer, more diffuse light replaced it. "And this." Another click and the light turned red and bright again.

"A triple-duty flashlight. Nice," she said as he switched it back to the soft light and set it on a shelf just beneath the counter. "Does it do any more tricks?"

"There's a button that will make it flash. And I found this." He held a tiny disc between his first finger and thumb. He pressed it.

"A laser beam. What are you going to do with that?"

He shrugged. "Who knows? It's neat, though, isn't it?"

She chuckled. "It is neat." She flicked her light on and off, then stuck it into the pocket of her jeans.

"We should be all set," he said. Then he put his light on the soft setting and pointed it at her face.

"Hey," she protested, squinting.

"You're kind of cute with your hair all wet and your raccoon eyes."

She swiped a finger below her eyes. It came away smudged with black. Great. Her mascara was running and she didn't have any makeup in her purse. Gun—yes. Makeup—no.

An odd little hiccup bubbled up from her throat, followed by another one and another. Tears ran down her cheeks, but she wasn't crying. Not exactly. She was laughing—kind of. She put her knuckles against her teeth. Was she becoming hysterical?

Harte frowned. "Are you okay?" he asked.

She shook her head and tried to stop the laughter that was bubbling up from her chest, but she couldn't. "I—I'm sorry," she stammered. "I—can't seem to—help it."

"It's okay," he said softly, wrapping his arm around her and pulling her close to his side.

She shivered at the warmth of his body.

"Now, what's so funny?"

"When you called me raccoon eyes, my first thought

was that I don't have any makeup in my purse." She could barely talk for the spasms of laughter.

Harte smiled. "Hard to believe, given the size of it."

She sniffed.

"You know, people react in different ways. Just let it out."

Her throat and chest quivered with the strange half laugh, half sob for a few more seconds. Then suddenly, it stopped. Dani hiccuped one more time. "That was weird," she said.

Harte's arm tightened around her shoulders, urging her to relax. She gave in and let herself sink into his side. She felt him put his lips against her hair, felt them move as he murmured gentle, comforting words. She couldn't hear everything he said, but that was okay. It was his strength, his warmth, his closeness that mattered.

Her muscles, cold and tired, twitched shakily. Each time her arm or leg jerked, he laid his palm on the twitching limb and rubbed it.

In an odd way, it reminded her of when she was a child. Tears choked her throat again. She coughed. "When I was little, my granddad would rub my legs when I woke up crying with the leg-ache," she said.

"You always lived with him after your dad died?"

She nodded. "My dad died when I was seven. So Granddad raised me."

"Where was your mom?" Harte asked, his breath stirring her hair.

"Gone. Since I was three."

"I'm sorry," he said.

Dani shook her head, but when she opened her mouth

to say, *It was a long time ago,* the words wouldn't come out. A little sob erupted from her throat, and tears filled her eyes. "Damn it," she muttered. "This is ridiculous. I never cry."

"Hey," Harte whispered, putting a finger under her chin and lifting her face to his. "Give yourself a break."

"A break? It's so stupid to cry. It doesn't help anything." She blotted her cheeks with her palms. "It's humiliating."

"I don't know a handful of people who could have dealt with everything that's happened as well as you have." His mouth quirked upward. "And you pick a mean lock."

"I do that," she said, trying to smile. A sob, like a tiny hiccup, escaped her lips.

"Shh." Harte touched the corner of her mouth with a finger, then bent his head and brushed a kiss across her cheek. It was so light it seemed hardly more than a breath.

But it was enough to reignite the fire he'd stoked inside her earlier, when she'd dared to kiss him. She felt the exquisite longing rise and flare again. She wanted to turn to him, open to him and beg him to wrap her in those strong, warm arms and make love to her. Her rational mind knew that giving in to the urge would be a big mistake, for so many reasons. She and Harte Delancey were at opposite ends of every spectrum she could think of—political, financial, social. He was ambitious, probably hoping to be D.A. one day. She'd become a public defender because she wanted to help people who would otherwise have no one on their side.

The only thing the two of them had in common was

the enemy that was after them. And while joining forces to fight a deadly enemy made good sense, it also made for strange bedfellows. Right here and now, though, she didn't care. She wanted closeness. She wanted comfort. She wanted assurance that no matter how desperate the situation, the two of them were still alive. And she wanted to feel something besides fear, at least for a little while.

He was unaware of the argument going on inside her, but he was not unaware of her. She knew it, and she used it. Turning, she settled closer into his arms. Reaching up a hand, she slid her fingers along the line of his jaw and back to caress his earlobe. His mouth was firm yet gentle as she touched her lips to his. Ignoring the voice in her head that was telling her what a bad idea it was to kiss him, she leaned in farther, opening her mouth to taste him better. The feel of his lips and tongue was so sweet and at the same time so titillating that hot new tears sprang to her eyes and her breath caught in a sob.

Harte froze for an instant, then pulled back. "Dani, I don't—" He stopped. His chest was heaving.

"No, I'm sorry. It's just everything." She felt tears welling up in her eyes. She willed them to stop, but it didn't help. They spilled down her wet cheeks, scalding them. "I promise you," she said with a choked laugh. "I almost never cry."

Harte sat back and held out his arm. Instinctively, Dani moved closer. For a brief moment, he didn't move, just sat there, his arm resting across her back. "I believe you," he said softly. "Makes my eyes red and gives me a headache."

He ran his palm down her bare shoulder to her upper arm. "You're cold."

"Not so much now," she murmured as she nestled into the shelter of his arm. "How do you stay so warm in nothing but a shirt?"

He shivered and laughed ruefully. "I don't."

"But your skin—it's always warm."

"Maybe warmer than yours. But that's because you're so skinny you can't hold any heat."

Dani chuckled as her tears dried on her cheeks. "Please. Don't try to butter me up. I am not skinny."

"No. You're not. At least not everywhere," he acceded. His palm caressed her shoulder and arm, sending shivers not caused by the temperature through her.

She snuggled a little closer to him. "Oh, I've never felt so helpless in my life," she murmured. "Except maybe the night Granddad died." That thought closed her throat and made her eyes sting. "Here I go again," she said, blotting the tears from her cheeks.

"Hey." He slid his fingers under her chin and urged her head up. "It's okay. No need to cry," he said, his thumb brushing across her cheek; then he pulled her closer.

His lips pressed against her forehead—warm, firm, steady. "No need to cry," he whispered again, the comforting words penetrating her heart and lighting all the dark, scary places inside her.

Right now he wasn't her rival or her attorney. She didn't want to put a name to what she was feeling right this minute. All she knew was that he was her port in the storm. He was strength and warmth and safety, and she needed that. She lifted her head, seeking more. His mouth moved from her temple to her cheek and then to her lips.

She moaned quietly.

He made a sound in his throat, bent his head and covered her mouth with his. This time it was no gentle, comforting kiss that made her question her reaction. His tongue slid along her parted lips and farther, to explore the inside of her mouth. The sensation turned her blood into molten lava that flowed through every part of her, changing her smoldering longing into searing desire.

He whispered her name as his fingers slipped up the nape of her neck and through her hair to cradle the back of her head. He went further, deepening the kiss, invading her mouth in an erotic mimicry of lovemaking. The sensual stroking of his tongue sent shivers of desire down, down, all the way to her core, feeding a hunger that nearly consumed her. She wanted him— needed him. She kissed him back greedily, amazed that his straight, firm mouth could feel so supple and gentle and at the same time so demanding.

She breathed in his scent, felt the rough stubble on his cheeks scrape her skin. He was deliciously male, solid and strong in a fascinating way that was so different from her own body. His arms and chest felt like steel wrapped in silk. Just as she reached up to wrap her hands around his neck and pull him closer, greedy for more of the breathtaking desire, he froze.

"What?" she said against his mouth, her heart jackhammering in her chest. "Did you hear something?"

"No," he rasped, his voice hoarse with emotion. He pulled away from her and leaned back against the wall.

"Then what? Is it me?" She winced as soon as the

words were out of her mouth. Even if that was why he had pulled away, she didn't want to know.

He gave his head a shake and rose to his haunches. "Harte?"

"Don't make something of nothing. You're soaking wet and you haven't stopped shivering. I'm pretty miserable too. We need to find some dry clothes and see what else is around here that we can use."

Dani wanted to tell him that yes, she was chilly, but her shivering was caused not by the weather, but by his kiss, his scent, the warmth of his skin. But before she could speak, he was pushing himself to his feet.

"And we can't forget that those guys are still out there, looking for us. Thank God they no longer have a car. But there are four of them." He turned his attention to the front windows for a moment, then wiped his face.

"I'll go see what I can find," he said in what she thought of as his prosecutor's tone—formal, a bit detached, professional. He could have been talking to anybody. Anybody except the person he'd just shared a hot, erotic kiss with.

It was clear as glass. He was sorry he'd kissed her—and she was very sorry about that.

Chapter Eleven

Harte cursed himself silently but fluently as he clenched his jaw and forced his breathing under control. How had he let that happen? Being so close to Dani was too enticing. He was apparently not capable of controlling himself around her.

He'd promised himself that he'd protect her. As her attorney, it was his duty. And in no dictionary did any definition of the word *protection* include seduction. He'd gotten her into this dangerous situation, and there was no way he was going to allow himself to be blinded by his raging attraction to her. Her safety, her life, depended on his self-control. It was important that both of them understood that.

He took a deep breath and turned back toward her, digging deep inside for the strength to face her dispassionately.

"Dani," he said tightly. "Your safety is my responsibility. If I'm going to protect you, you're going to have to help me. We need each other's warmth and support, and it's natural that our closeness might lead to—tension."

He stood and looked down at her, his expression grim. "But I can't let anything happen between us. If

I let my guard down for even a minute, it could get you killed."

Mortification flooded her face, and her cheeks flamed. His heart ached to pull her into his arms and assure her that he desired her, but it was better for her to think he didn't want her than to risk her safety.

"I'm aware of the danger," she said archly.

"I know you are."

"And I understand what you're saying. I suppose you're right. It is the normal male reaction—"

"That's not what I said."

Dani held up her hand. "It's all right. We're in a deadly, dangerous situation and the only way we're going to survive is if we can depend on each other to be strong. I didn't mean to distract you."

"Damn it, Dani. I'm trying to keep us alive. This is not personal." Hell. That hadn't come out right. He'd gone about this all wrong, and she was not helping. If she'd just stop and think, surely she'd realize what he meant. Irritation flared inside him.

"Just try to stay focused, okay?" he said, and turned to shine the flashlight toward the main floor of the store.

Dani could see the muscle in his jaw working. His chiseled features looked sculpted in marble. She watched as he withdrew, physically and emotionally. His back was ramrod straight, the muscles knotted. His whole body exuded intense control.

What she'd told him was true. She knew he was right. They had to stay focused. Distractions could be deadly. Harte might have lost his focus for an instant to indulge his lust, but now Mr. Prosecutor was back.

"I'll be right back," he said, just as lightning flashed and thunder roared.

Dani jumped and gasped. "Where are you going?" she asked anxiously.

Harte heard the apprehension in her voice. It reminded him that, as brave as she'd been, she was deeply afraid of storms.

"I just want to check things out." He turned to look out the glass front of the drugstore as another bolt of lightning flared. The thunder seemed to be roiling continuously. The rain and wind made it almost impossible to see anything, and all the lightning did was to brighten the grays.

"I don't think they will suspect that we're here. I couldn't see inside from out there."

She turned to look, and cringed when a flash of lightning flared, followed immediately by a clap of thunder. "Why isn't the storm moving away?"

"I guess that low front stalled it."

"I guess." Dani's voice was a mixture of apprehension and weariness.

Harte picked up the big flashlight and shone the narrow beam on the signs about the aisles of shelves. "Batteries, aisle four," he read. "Stationery, toys, paper towels. Looks like we've got all the comforts of home." He turned the flashlight in the opposite direction. "Ah, kitchen," he said, and headed in that direction.

"Kitchen?"

"Sure. I want some towels to dry off with. As soon as I get them, I want to find an elastic bandage."

He grabbed some dish towels. "These should work," he said, and tucked them under his arm.

Dani was reading the signs on the other aisles. "Look, Harte," she cried. "T-shirts."

They picked out long-sleeved T-shirts that read The Big Easy. "And hoodies!" Dani cried. "Ooh—fleece."

His heart twisted painfully in his chest at the look on her face. She beamed as if the fleece were golden. It took all his self-control not to hug her tight and promise her he'd make it his personal mission to see that she never felt cold again.

"Here," he said, spotting fleece throws. He grabbed two. "These will be good if we get chilly."

"I wish they had pants," she said wistfully. "Although these jeans are hard enough to get on and off dry. I'll probably never be able to peel them off soaking wet."

Harte couldn't help looking as she held up a pink hoodie with a graffiti design, measuring it against her. *Tight* didn't begin to describe her jeans, now that they were wet. They looked as though they'd been painted on her sexy hips and legs. He loved her body. It was curvy in all the right places and in precisely the right amount. He swallowed hard and did his best not to get lost in an image of her wiggling her way out of those wet jeans.

"Harte, look!" she cried.

He turned. She'd gone to the end of the aisle and was reading the signs farther along. "Scrubs and socks—and oh, thank God, underwear."

She ran. When he caught up, she handed him a pair of scrubs. "Here's a pair of XL for you and a medium for me." She headed up the aisle to a display of socks, boxers and briefs and panties. She grabbed a package of cotton panties and one of socks, then paused. She looked up at him. Her face held a pained expression. "We're looting, aren't we?"

"I guess so, in the strictest sense of the word. But I'll bet the owner wouldn't begrudge us these few items, under the circumstances." He gave her a small smile. "If it makes you feel better, I'll send him a check when we get out of here."

"When we get out—" she echoed, then turned toward him, doubt and fear darkening her eyes. "Swear to me that we will get out of here."

"Of course we will," he said, unable to resist reaching out to touch her cheek and berating himself for his weakness. A fluttery feeling rippled in his chest when her head inclined toward his hand. "As soon as we've rested for a few minutes, we need to get out of here and get as far away from this area as we can. As soon as I figure out what street we're on, I'll be able to find a police station."

She lifted her head and gave him a searching gaze. "A police station. Really?"

"Really," he assured her. He wished he was as confident as he sounded. "Now we need to get out of these wet clothes."

A sudden blast of wind rattled the windows and doors and made the roof creak loudly. It roared like an oncoming train. Dani threw herself into Harte's arms with a small shriek. He held on to her until the noise died down.

"I'm so sorry. I'm trying not to react every time it thunders," she said as she picked up the items she'd dropped.

"You're doing real well."

"You don't think that was a tornado, do you?"

He shook his head. "It sounded more like straight-line wind. But I wouldn't be surprised if some of the damage we've seen and heard has been from tornadoes. These spring storms can spawn them."

"I know," Dani muttered.

Harte cringed, his heart aching with understanding. Her father had died in a tornado. Of course she was terrified that any wind and rain would turn into a deadly funnel cloud. He shouldn't have gone on and on about them.

"There's the pain-relief aisle. I need an elastic bandage for my ankle. Then we can check out the back." He grabbed a bandage and headed toward the back of the store.

"There," he said, pointing toward a door that said Employees Only. When he opened it, he found a dark, musty storeroom with shelves groaning under the weight of boxes and bins of all shapes and sizes. There was a door marked with an Exit sign.

Throwing the latch on the exit door, he eased it open. The rain was still coming down in buckets, and the alley behind the store was running at least six inches deep in water. He set his jaw and stuck his head out, wincing at the chilly wind that blew rain in his face. He'd almost dried enough that he didn't feel waterlogged. He wasn't anxious to get out into the rain again. But he'd needed to check out their means of escape. "We can get out this way if we need to," he said, closing and latching the door.

Dani sighed. "Okay. Can we go back inside the store?

It's chilly out here. And look." She pointed. "The roof is leaking like a sieve."

"Sure, go ahead," Harte said. "I'll change in here. Take some of these towels."

"Stand over here near the door while you're changing," she said. "Otherwise your clothes will be wet again before you get them on."

She left and Harte quickly shed his shirt and peeled off his jeans, remembering what she'd said about hers. She was right. The wet denim felt like duct tape as he peeled them down his legs. He dried off quickly and donned the scrub pants. Then he sat on one haunch as he quickly and efficiently wrapped his sore and swollen ankle and pulled on clean dry socks. But once it was wrapped, he found that he couldn't get his shoe back on. He tried the bandage alone, but no. It was still too large. Finally, sighing with frustration and the anticipation of more pain, he unwrapped his foot and tossed the bandage aside. He was able to get the shoe on over a dry sock. Just as he reached for the long-sleeved Big Easy T-shirt, he heard a crash and a scream.

Grabbing the flashlight, he bolted through the door and almost ran headlong into a shelf. Careering around it, he sprinted to the front of the store. "Dani? Dani!"

He heard her whimper.

Turning toward her voice, he saw the narrow beam of her flashlight canted across the floor, illuminating a pale body sprawled on the floor. "Dani!"

She was sprawled facedown on the floor with her wet jeans and a pair of white panties tangled around her feet, and scrubs and hoodie in a pile beside her. She was wearing nothing but the T-shirt. *Nothing* but the T-shirt. Her pale, shapely backside was bare.

He blinked and clamped his jaw tight. "Dani—" he said, and started to bend down. Thank God there was at least one part of his brain that was holding on to rational thought, even though the rest of him was reacting to the exquisite sight of her beautiful, bare body.

"No!" She turned her head and looked up at him, horrified. "Get away!"

He froze.

She wriggled as she tried to pull the tail of the shirt down to cover her butt. She wasn't successful. "Go— somewhere, please," she begged. "Don't look."

Harte didn't know what to do except turn his back.

"Are you hurt?"

"No," she said shortly.

He heard fabric rustling and a couple of quiet groans of frustration.

"So you tripped over your jeans when you tried to take them off?" he asked, trying his best to sound serious and supportive, although in a different situation, it would be really funny.

"Don't you dare laugh at me. I swear I'll—" She yelped in pain.

Harte whirled. She was holding her left wrist. "What is it?" he asked. "Your wrist?"

"Don't look," she cried. "Turn around!"

"I need to look at your wrist."

"It's fine," she said. The stubborn tightness of her voice was in sharp contrast to the mortified and pain-filled look on her face. She raised her gaze to his. "Please."

He turned his back again. While he waited for her to dress, he occupied himself by trying, without much success, to banish the vision of her exquisite curves. He heard her moving around. Then she bit off another gasp of pain.

He almost turned around, but he restrained himself. "Be careful with your wrist. If it's broken—"

"I am," she grated. He could practically hear her jaw clenching. After a few moments, she said, "Okay. I'm dressed."

He turned around and looked at her. But she was looking at the pile of clothes on the floor, and her face was turning bright red.

He looked down to see what was so embarrassing for her. There, nice and white and pretty, were the cotton bikini panties she'd found on the store shelves. He stared at the dazzling white scrap of fabric lying on the drugstore floor, every bit as mesmerized as she'd been, and certain he was thinking the same thing she was. He raised his gaze to hers and felt himself grow hard at the thought that she had nothing on under the thin cotton scrub pants.

She swallowed audibly and drew in a long breath.

Harte waited, wondering what she was going to say, because he had no idea what he should do.

"I—guess I forgot something," she said hoarsely.

Harte felt his face burn. He let go of a huge breath that he hadn't realized he was holding. "Yeah," he said, his gaze flickering toward the panties, then back to meet hers. "Yeah."

After a long moment, he cleared his throat. "Let me see your wrist. I need to make sure it's not broken."

"Okay," she said meekly.

He realized he was still holding the flashlight, so he set it down on the counter. It was on the soft-light setting and he aimed it toward the wall, hoping the light and its reflection would help him see. Swallowing hard, fighting for control over his libido, he bent down next to her and gently took her forearm in his hands and examined it closely.

While he studied her wrist, Dani took the opportunity to study him. With his head down, his profile was lit by the faint light of the flashlight. He was undeniably good-looking. She already knew that. But she hadn't realized just how classic his features were. His nose was long and straight, his mouth was firm, his jawline was chiseled. And those eyes—she could actually see the shadow of his lashes on his cheek.

"How'd you hit it?" he asked as he used her flashlight to inspect the wrist bone.

"Hmm?" Was it fair for one man to be so beautiful from so many different angles?

"Dani?"

She blinked. What had he said? "What?"

"Are you sure you're all right? You didn't hit your head, did you?"

"No, I didn't hit my head. I think my wrist hit the edge of the counter when I tripped. And it was already sore from when I jumped up onto the porch."

He nodded. "It's a little red, but I don't see any swelling or discoloration."

His touch was so gentle, his voice so kind that it made her want to cry—because apparently, she was going to cry about *everything* from now on. And once they managed to get away from these men who seemed determined to kill them, she could tell she was in for a long jag.

With a quick shake of her head, she bit down on her cheek and blinked away the stinging behind her eyelids.

"Does it hurt when I move it?" he asked, manipulating it tenderly.

"No," she said. "It really doesn't hurt any more or any less. It just aches."

"It's probably strained. Try getting up. See if you can put weight on it."

She stood without a problem. "It's fine," she said, but when she looked up at him, she found that he'd stepped close, ready to catch her if she faltered.

"Are you sure—?" He stopped talking when their gazes met. His mouth was less than an inch from hers. She looked at his lips, then back up into his eyes. His gaze was dark, his eyes smoky. "Dani—" he started.

At that instant, the front windows rattled and something crashed into the door. Dani screamed just as Harte caught her in his arms and dove to the floor.

Chapter Twelve

A roar like a freight train filled the air, and the windows rattled more loudly. Dani lay shielded by Harte's strong body. His hands covered her head protectively, and his cheek rested against hers. His long, rock-solid thighs were splayed across hers, his hard, heavy arousal pressing against her belly.

The wind roared and whistled, slinging trash and shingles and tree branches against buildings. She lay there, shielded by his body, as the tornado—because she knew without a doubt that it was a tornado—passed over them. Finally, the deafening noise died down.

Harte wasted no time pushing himself off her, and she knew why. She'd felt his arousal. Her cheeks grew warm. No matter how he felt about her, she knew he did desire her. He just didn't want to.

"That was bad," she whispered.

"Stay still," he said. Without looking at her, he rose and looked out the windows. He whistled under his breath. "Lots of damage," he said. "I see a couple of bicycle tires, twisted spokes." He craned his neck. "I think that big crash was a screen door hitting the windows. There's a huge crack in the window on the left.

I'd expect the bulletproof glass to stay intact, but I'm amazed that all the windows didn't shatter."

"That was a tornado," she said, wishing she could stop imagining deadly funnel clouds roaring toward them, sucking up everything in their paths. When the wind had been at its worst, it had sounded like a freight train.

He yawned exaggeratedly, popping his ears. "I think so. It's so quiet it feels weird."

"I don't hear any sirens."

Harte shook his head. "With this much debris and damage everywhere, the city will be focusing all its manpower toward clearing major thoroughfares and routes to hospitals for emergency vehicles."

"At least we're all right."

He nodded as he pulled his cell phone from his pocket and checked it. "Hey! I've got bars!" he exclaimed. "Two bars."

Dani's heart leaped into her throat. "Call 911!" she exclaimed.

He paused in the act of pressing a button. "They can't get to us. They probably can't keep up with the injuries in the busier parts of the city. I'm calling Lucas." He pressed a button and listened. "Oh, come on," he muttered. Then his eyes lit up. "I'm getting through."

Dani's eyes stung. Finally, this awful nightmare would be over.

"Lucas!" Harte yelled. "Lucas, can you hear me?" He stepped out from behind the counter and moved toward the front of the store, checking the signal every few steps.

"Yeah, it's Harte. I know, the connection does suck,

but listen…" He paused. "Lucas? You still there?" Then he walked the line of the windows, from one side of the store to the other.

Dani held her breath, as if that would help hold together the fragile connection.

"Damn it, don't fade on me now," Harte said, then spoke loudly and distinctly. "Lucas, we're at Delaughter's Drugs, near Religious. Repeat—Delaughter's Drugs. Pursued by armed men. Repeat—armed men." He listened for a few seconds. "Lucas?" Then he threw his head back and growled.

"Do you think he heard you?" Dani asked.

Harte was frowning at his phone. "I don't know."

Dani fished down into her purse, her fingers brushing the cold steel of the SIG as she searched for her phone. She knew she needed to tell Harte about the gun, but she'd waited too long. She had no doubt how he'd react, and she dreaded the prosecutorial lecture she'd have to endure when he found out she'd been packing this whole time. She found her phone and pulled it out. It showed one bar. "Let's send a text." If the phone managed to get the text sent, then Lucas would at least see it once service was restored.

Harte nodded. "I'll send it to Lucas and Ethan." He quickly entered a message. In Delaughter's Drugs near B & B, hiding from armed men. Send help! He pressed Send and pocketed his phone. "Give me yours. I'll send the same text. That'll be two service providers—two chances for it to get through."

Another loud rattling of the windows announced the wind picking up again. Harte grabbed Dani and pulled her down behind the counter. "We need to be careful.

One of these gusts of wind is likely to throw something hard enough at those windows to break them."

They sat together, shoulder to shoulder. Dani closed her eyes, basking in the heat Harte's body gave off and trying to pretend that she didn't want him to pull her close and make hot, sweet love to her. But as much as she wanted him deep inside her, she craved his warmth and strength surrounding her even more. When he held her in his arms, she felt as if nothing could harm her.

"Harte? Where do you think they are—the men?"

She felt his shoulders rise and fall. "No telling. I tried to keep up with which direction and how far we ran from the warehouse. I think we made it about ten blocks. That's a big circle they've got to search."

"And you're sure they were sent by Yeoman?"

"Don't know who else it would be. Like I said before, I think Stamps would have more sense. Yeoman, on the other hand, deals in physical force. It's what he knows."

"It doesn't make any sense. Why would he think killing me would solve his problem?"

Harte assessed her. "You're the only person who can connect him with your grandfather's murder. In his world, shooting you is the easiest way to get rid of you. It's incredibly hard to prove somebody shot somebody without an eyewitness."

She shivered and Harte immediately put his arm around her.

"Cold?"

His heat soaked into her, making her feel aroused and languid at the same time. "A little," she said, "but mostly, I can't shake the feeling that they're right behind me, breathing down my neck." She shivered again.

"Should we be doing something—getting farther away maybe?"

Harte didn't speak for a moment. He ran his palm up and down her arm. "I wondered about that. If Lucas or Ethan gets my message, they'll come here." He settled back against the wall and tightened his hold on her. "Look at it from those goons' point of view. They're looking for a needle in a haystack. And that car can't be drivable after they rammed it into that freight door three times."

"So they're on foot, just like us. I guess that's a good thing."

"And like I said, they've got an awfully big area to search, and they have to search every building on each and every street."

"They know which door we went out."

"Yeah, but we made at least two right turns. We couldn't see anything, which means they couldn't either. If they'd been able to see us, they'd have shot at us."

The wind rose again, whistling around corners and roaring past the broken door. "Here we go again," he said. Rain pelted the glass windows, flung there by the whipping winds.

"Those windows are going to break eventually," she said.

"They might," he agreed, "but that's why I put us here in the cashier's cage. It's metal, bolted down and we've got bulletproof glass protecting us." He gave her arm a reassuring squeeze.

"Okay," she said, not sounding convinced.

"Hey," Harte said. "Trust me."

She snuggled in closer to his side. Harte held her

and listened to the storm. He could feel the tension in her stiff limbs, her fingers that were curved into a fist against his skin, her shaky breaths.

Lightning flashed almost continuously and the roar of the thunder and wind was near deafening. Above their heads, a vicious screech overrode the sound of the storm.

Dani jumped. Harte cupped the back of her head and pressed it to his chest, resting his cheek against her hair. "It's okay," he murmured, although he doubted she could hear him. "It's going to be okay."

He risked a glance upward, fully expecting to see that part of the roof had blown off, taking the ceiling with it. The screeching had sounded like nails being ripped out. But the ceiling appeared intact. With all the rain and wind, they'd know soon enough if the roof was damaged.

Then, as quickly as it had started, the roaring stopped. The lightning was no longer continuous and the thunder seemed farther away.

Dani didn't relax a bit. Now that things had calmed down, he could feel her trembling.

"Listen," he said. "I think the worst is over." He took his hand away from the back of her head and touched her chin. "Look at me, Dani."

Slowly, haltingly, she raised her head. "I—I'm sorry," she muttered.

"For what? For being scared? I was scared too."

She shuddered. "Not like me." She sighed. "My father died more than twenty years ago and I'm still acting like a child."

After a long time, she lifted her head. Harte looked

down at her. "You okay?" he whispered, giving her a little smile.

She nodded, then dropped her gaze to his mouth. "Harte—?"

He looked at her parted lips, her soft whiskey-colored eyes.

"Dani," he said, "I don't think—"

"Don't think," Dani whispered, and brushed his lips with hers. She meant that admonition for herself as well as him. He'd held her and sheltered her. He'd protected her from the storm.

Sighing, she kissed him again. This time she touched his mouth with the tip of her tongue.

She wasn't thinking about what would happen once they were safe. Right now she wanted him with an ache that had been growing ever since he'd kissed her that first time.

He didn't move a muscle.

She withdrew and turned away, pressing her knuckles against her teeth. A short unamused laugh escaped her throat. "Sorry," she said tightly. "It takes me a while, but eventually I get the picture."

He closed his eyes and shook his head.

She cleared her throat. "I apologize. I guarantee it won't happen ag—"

He pulled her back to him. His mouth came down on hers hard, his tongue parting her lips.

Dani gasped as he deepened the kiss. The ache inside her turned to a tingling thrill that surged through her like a lightning bolt.

He moaned deep in his throat and lifted her onto

his lap. The only thing between them was two layers of thin cotton.

"Still think I don't want you?" Harte muttered against her lips as he pushed his fingers through her damp hair and kissed her again, more fiercely than before. "Don't ever make that mistake again."

Any doubt she might have had disappeared into a silver haze of desire. His arousal pressed insistently against her, stirring her blood to a fever pitch as he slid his hands under the T-shirt and pushed it up. She raised her arms so he could pull it over her head.

His hands moved on her skin, trailing sparks like a wizard everywhere they touched. Her waist, her rib cage, the soft skin beneath her breasts. Finally, with exquisite slowness, he trailed his fingertips over the swell of her breasts until she arched, pressing them into his hands.

He skimmed his thumbs across her nipples. They puckered immediately and throbbed, they were so sensitive.

His kisses were sweet and erotic at the same time. One instant his tongue sparred with hers in a sensual dance that almost sent her over the edge. The next, he withdrew, only to return and plant light, unbearably sweet butterfly kisses onto every square millimeter of her mouth, cheeks and eyelids.

Just as she thought she couldn't feel any more turned on, he bent his head and took a nipple into his mouth. He teased it with his tongue, then grazed it lightly with his teeth. A tight, choked scream erupted from her throat. Every touch sent electric shocks across her nerve endings from her fingers to her toes to her very core. He licked the tiny nub until it was wet, then lightly blew on it until Dani thought she would scream with pleasure. Then he turned to lavish the same attention on the other breast.

"Harte," she rasped. "I can't stand any more—" Her words were cut short by his rumble of soft laughter.

"You're going to have to," he said. He ran his palm down her body to the drawstring of the scrub pants. He untied it, then slid the material down over her hips and past her knees. She kicked them off, leaving her completely naked.

She didn't care. She twisted until she straddled him, then leaned down and gave him back the kisses he'd given her. Putting her hands on his bare chest, she used her fingertips on his nipples, teasing them to instant arousal and drawing a pained moan from his throat.

"Do you like that?" she asked as she teased the erect tips unrelentingly.

"No—" he gasped, taking hold of her wrists. His arousal pulsed against her, belying his words.

Harte arched, thrusting upward in unfettered response to her playing with his nipples. It was an unfamiliar, slightly uncomfortable sensation, and yet each touch arrowed straight down to his throbbing arousal.

She peered at him from under her lashes, a seductive smile on her face, and then twisted her wrists out of his clutches. Placing her palms on his chest, she bent and kissed him again.

"Slow down," he muttered, "or it's going to all be over."

"I don't want to slow down," she whispered in response. "I want you in me, now."

"Too soon," he protested. "You're not ready." As he spoke, he slid his hand down over her belly to the slight rise of her mound.

"Yes, I am," Dani gasped, so turned on by the twin pressures of his hand and his arousal against her that she could barely breathe, much less speak.

When he curled his fingers into the patch of hair that hid her sexual center, then slowly, gently, slid a finger between her soft, sensitized folds, she cried out, certain she was going to faint. He pressed into her, testing her readiness to receive him.

Her thighs tightened involuntarily, whether to hold on to the sensations he was stirring or to slow down the inevitable explosive conclusion, she didn't know. She was becoming lost in erotic ecstasy.

"Yes, you are," he whispered.

In answer, she lifted herself and guided him into her. He pushed carefully and steadily until he was buried inside her. She moaned and threw her head back, losing herself in a climax that went on and on.

Harte felt Dani's delicately intense contractions, and they triggered his own. With his breaths sawing in his throat and his muscles and sinews straining, he came, driving into her welcoming body as she met him, thrust for thrust.

Finally, drained, he collapsed back against the wall and Dani melted, as if boneless, atop him.

Chapter Thirteen

After a long time, Dani felt Harte lift her off him and set her gently down on the fleece blanket, then stretch out beside her. She didn't open her eyes. She didn't want to face reality yet. Her entire being was still floating on an ethereal cloud of fantasy.

A fantasy where there were no storms, no thunder, no soaking, pounding rain, where the sun was warm and bright, where no bad guys were chasing her and where the man with whom she'd just shared sweet, erotic sex would still want her once the danger was over. But trying to preserve the fantasy was a fruitless effort. She could feel reality hovering, looking for a way in. The reality of their separate lives—hers as a public defender who had to live on a government salary, and his as an assistant D.A. who was wealthy in his own right. They lived and worked in two different worlds.

Harte spread something over her, the pink hoodie maybe, then slid his arm under her head and shifted so she could rest her head on his shoulder. It helped a little. But reality was still out there, lurking.

She had to open her eyes sometime, and when she did, she'd be defenseless against the surge of regrets that were waiting to hit her. How many mistakes had

she made when she let that one careless second pass—
that one instant during which she could have made the
decision *not* to kiss him?

First and foremost, she'd exposed herself to him—
physically, yes. But also emotionally. The thing she'd
vowed not to do. For her, sex was not a casual romp.
It was too intimate, too exquisitely satisfying, to take
for granted. She never took it lightly and she'd never
had regrets.

Until now. Once they got out of here, she knew she'd
never be able to face Harte in court again. She could
picture him now, standing before the judge in one of his
impeccably tailored suits, with his expensive briefcase
and a knowing smile as she walked into the courtroom.
Her face burned just thinking about it.

She might have been able to work with him if all
they'd done was kiss. She'd still be fascinated by him,
still be amazed at how one person could be so unrelentingly gorgeous and sexy. But now they'd made love,
and Dani knew she'd never be the same. What had
been a silly office crush was no longer silly or just a
crush to her.

She'd just put herself on a fast track to a broken
heart. And she didn't even want to think what her
granddad would say if he knew. She moaned silently.

"Dani?"

Harte's soft voice startled her. Her eyes flew open
and met his dark gaze.

"Hey," he said, smiling. "I guess you were asleep. I
thought you said something."

Dani lifted her head from his shoulder and scooted

backward, holding the hoodie in place over her breasts and thighs.

He leaned up on one elbow.

"No, no," she said. "I didn't say anything." She wanted to sit up, to take some sort of control, at least of her body's position, but the hoodie wasn't big enough to cover everything she wanted covered. Any move she made would expose something.

"So I did wake you," he said. "Sorry."

She kept shaking her head. "You didn't wake me at all. No. I was awake already. I didn't go to sleep. I was just—" She stopped, clamping her jaw. She was babbling. "I need to—get dressed.

Harte held her gaze for a beat as something shadowed behind his eyes, and then he nodded. "Sure. Give me a second." He rolled away and sat up with his back to her, straightening and tying the drawstring waist of his scrub pants.

Without turning around he said, "I'm going to take a look around. See how much more damage the storm has done. See if anyone's moving around outside."

Dani's face burned like fire as she looked around for the panties she'd forgotten to put on earlier. She'd let him take all her clothes off, strip her naked. And he'd never even dropped his pants, just opened them. Like a quickie. She grimaced and her hot face got even hotter.

To him, she'd been a quickie. Mortified, her cheeks burning and her eyes stinging, she glanced over to be sure he wasn't looking, then pulled on the panties and grabbed the scrub pants. She held the hoodie against her breasts as she took off in the direction of the storeroom.

Harte shook his head as he heard her padding quickly

toward the back of the store. He'd never claimed to understand women. The things they did never ceased to befuddle him.

Sex with Dani had been better than he could have imagined. Her body was exquisite. Sleek and smooth, enticingly curvy where a woman should be. He'd been entranced with the mix of eagerness and shyness she'd displayed. Then there was their lightning-fast, nearly simultaneous climax. Her immediate, sensual response had surprised him.

His own hair-trigger climax had blown his mind.

Both of them had collapsed afterward, drained. He'd felt sapped, and had basked in the afterglow with Dani's soft hair against his shoulder and chest as her soft breaths echoed in his ear. He'd thought she was basking too. But despite her seeming boneless as she'd collapsed against him when he'd pulled her close and rested her head on his shoulder, she'd acted embarrassed and escaped as soon as she could.

She didn't strike him as one of those women who was embarrassed about her body. Shy maybe. He shrugged. That could be it, he supposed.

Now that she had run to the back of the store, he came back around the counter and looked for the long-sleeved T-shirt she'd found for him. Then he remembered. It was in the storeroom. He'd dropped it when she'd screamed.

Not wanting to disturb her, he headed toward the racks of T-shirts to find another one. Just as he got to the rack, she opened the storeroom door and came out. She was dressed in the scrub pants, the Big Easy T-shirt, the pink hoodie and her wet sneakers. She stopped short

when she saw him. Her gaze skittered down his torso to
the drawstring on the scrub pants, then back up.

She blinked. "Here—here's your T-shirt." She held
it out for him.

"Great, thanks," he said. He took the shirt by the
tail, shook it out once, then pulled it over his head and
down. A slight shiver went through him. He ran his
palms down each sleeve, then down his torso. "That
feels good," he said, meeting her gaze.

She looked away. "These wet shoes don't."

"Yeah," he said, looking down at his own wet loaf-
ers. "I know." He patted the pockets of the scrubs.
"Where's my phone?" he muttered. "I must have left
it in my jeans."

She moved out of the way of the storeroom door.
"Your jeans are on the floor," she said, then headed
toward the front of the store.

Harte quickly retrieved his phone and followed her.
"Damn it," he said when he checked the display. "No
reception."

Dani pulled her phone from her purse. "Oh, I have
a voice message," she cried.

Harte moved to where he could look over her shoulder. "From Lucas?" he asked.

"Don't know. I'll put it on Speaker." She pressed a
button on the phone and they listened.

*"We're sorry, you cannot access voice mail at this
time. Please try again later."*

"Great," Harte said, checking his display again.
"Yep. Zero bars. I thought maybe since the storm had
passed over, we'd be able to call for help."

Dani dropped the phone back into her big purse.

She raised her head, then suddenly moved away from him. It was as if she'd just realized how close he was standing to her. She still hadn't looked directly at him.

For once, he was sure he understood *this* woman perfectly. She regretted sleeping with him.

"Listen, Dani—"

"So, what now?" she interrupted, and immediately bit her lip. Her cheeks turned pink. "I mean, now that the storm is over, should we get out of here? Try to get to a police station or something?"

Harte turned to look out the front windows. "Yeah. The sun's going to come up soon. I'm going to go out and scout around."

"Then I'm going with you," she said.

"No. It's too dangerous. We could run into those men any second."

Dani propped her hands on her hips. "Exactly. Or a utility truck or a policeman. You'd have to come back and get me. That's just dumb."

Harte winced. She was right and she knew it. He could tell, because she gave a little nod of her head. Not much, just enough to say *So there*.

"Get ready to go," he said, then pointed his finger at her. "But I'm checking around the building first. You're not stepping one foot out of here until I'm sure the coast is clear."

"You're not going out there unarmed."

"What do you suggest I use? Your lock picks? Or maybe a water gun from the toy aisle?" he shot back.

With a look designed to wither him where he stood, she dug into her purse and pulled out—

"What the hell is that?" he snapped, staring at her hand.

She gave a short laugh. "It's a gun," she said with mock patience. "A SIG Sauer, to be specific."

"Where'd you get that?" he demanded. "Have you had it this whole time? Banging around in that—" He gestured. "Do you know how dangerous that is?"

She flushed, but not with embarrassment. She was angry. He could tell by the fire in her eyes and the lift of her chin.

"Yes," she snapped. "I know exactly how dangerous it is. Granddad gave it to me *and* taught me how to use it and care for it. You don't think for one minute that he would be so careless as to give me a weapon without making sure I could handle it?"

"How would I know what your grandfather would do?" Harte said irritably. "I do know this. Apparently, he skipped some basic precautions—like having enough respect for your partner to inform him that you're *packing* sometime within, say, the first eight hours or so of running for your lives."

Dani's face drained of color.

He realized immediately what he'd said. "Dani—I wasn't trying to insult your granddad—"

"You go to hell," she grated, then turned and stomped away. Her slender shoulders in the too-big hoodie were stiff and straight; her walk was regal.

Harte sighed in frustration and wiped a hand across his stubbled cheeks and chin. He'd crossed the line with his rude comment about her grandfather.

Hell, he'd crossed more lines in the past few hours than he ever had in his life. Insulting Freeman Canto wasn't the worst thing he'd done by far. No, the worst was forgetting his vow to keep Dani safe. He'd given in to the explosive attraction between them and taken advantage of her.

And now they were back to square one. Just like the day they'd faced off in court. Rivals, even enemies, in every sense of the word. The fragile trust he'd built with her by vowing to keep her safe had been strained by their lovemaking, but now he'd shattered that trust. And it could get Dani killed. Because they were going to have to make a run for it.

He glanced at his watch. Almost six o'clock in the morning. Any minute now the sun would start lightening the sky. That was good and bad. They'd be able to see street signs and landmarks, but it also meant they'd be visible. Reluctantly, he had to admit that he was relieved that they had a weapon. But they needed more than one.

What kind of weapon could he find in a drugstore? Pepper spray or a knife? He hoped like hell the men chasing them would not get close enough that Dani or he would need either of those.

"Harte!" Dani cried.

He rushed toward the front of the store and saw Dani crouched down behind the counter. "What is it?" he hissed.

She gestured at him. "Down! Get down! I saw something moving out there. I think it's them," she whispered urgently. "What are we going to do?"

"You saw them? What did you see?"

"I noticed the three-way flashlight was still on. I reached across the counter to turn it off and I saw dark shapes moving across the street."

The flashlight. It had been on the soft setting, but

still. What a stupid, potentially fatal mistake. From the street, the faint light probably looked like a beacon—the only speck of brightness in the unrelenting gray. He'd led their pursuers straight to them, because he'd let himself get distracted by his desire for Dani.

"At least you got it turned off."

"They must have seen it," she said shakily. "They know where we are."

"Not for certain. And we don't know for sure it's them." He laid his hand on her forearm. "But if it is, it won't take them five minutes to find the back door. Follow me and stay down."

They headed to the back, keeping low. When Harte opened the storeroom door, he saw that part of the roof had blown off and several pieces of rafters and broken plywood boards had fallen. He was glad they hadn't stayed back there.

"Stay here. I'm going to check and see if the coast is clear."

"Take the gun," Dani said, pressing it into his hand.

"No," he protested. "I'm not that good a shot."

"We know they have guns," she countered. "If they're already back here, this gun may be our only chance. If you won't take it, then move. I'll go out and see if the coast is clear."

He took it reluctantly, felt for the safety and thumbed it off. "What size magazine do you have in it?"

"Seventeen shots."

He nodded, then, bracing himself, pushed the door open—or tried to. It felt stuck. What the hell? His pulse hammered. Had they already made it around back and blocked the door? He pushed harder and heard a scraping sound. Through the tiny crack he saw a purple glow. Early dawn. The sky was just bright enough to make the shadows darker.

He slid the door open a bit more, grimacing at the noise made by whatever was blocking it. He was pretty sure he knew what it was. It was big, and had a distinctive hollow sound as it scraped on the ground. It was a plastic trash can—the thick, industrial size.

Finally, he'd managed to move the can enough so he could look around. Then he ducked back in. "I don't see anything. We need to run while we've got the chance."

"Okay," Dani said. "Which direction?"

"Straight back, between the two buildings right behind here. I've got to find the name of that street. Then maybe I can figure out where we are."

She nodded.

"Ready?" he asked.

"Ready."

Dani held her breath as Harte pushed open the door and went through it. She held on to the edge of the door for a couple of seconds. Once it closed, it would lock and they would have no place to hide. They could be picked off like plastic ducks at a carnival.

Harte gestured for her to wait. He quickly surveyed the alley, then moved forward cautiously. "Now," he whispered.

Dani felt a prickling on the nape of her neck. It reminded her of when she was a child and had to go into a dark room. Just like back then, and in the dark Mardi Gras float warehouse, she felt as if monsters were breathing down her neck.

In front of her, Harte's wide shoulders gave her a

measure of confidence. He believed they'd be fine, and she realized *she* believed him. She trusted him.

Ten minutes before, when he'd tossed out that unkind remark about her granddad, she'd painted him with the same brush as his father and grandfather. Everything she'd ever heard about the Delanceys depicted them as ambitious, ruthless and violent. Con Delancey had died violently, and Harte's dad, Robert, was rumored to have as violent a temper as Con.

But every time they were in a dangerous situation, Harte had protected her, so she felt confident and, yes, safe, as she stepped off the concrete stoop into the ankle-deep water that covered the pockmarked and cracked asphalt. Immediately, the cold water seeped through her already damp sneakers to soak her feet. Grimacing, she ignored it and followed him.

Just as they reached the center of the alley and Harte pointed to the left side of the building in front of them, Dani heard a noise. She couldn't tell what direction it had come from.

Harte's head snapped to the right. He'd heard it too.

Before she could even begin to decide how to react, he'd grabbed her upper arm and pulled her forward and down behind a stack of tires.

A loud pop echoed in her ears as she dropped to her knees, her fall partially broken by Harte's body. Her brain clicked into instant-replay mode and she realized that just prior to the pop, she'd heard a zinging sound near her ear—way too near.

"Are you hit?" Harte demanded, his hand still on her arm in a punishing grip.

"No," she panted. "You?"

He gave a negative jerk of his head. "Go!" he said. "Run to that alley and keep running."

"Not without you."

Another bullet whistled past them, then another.

"Dani, go! I'm right behind you."

She met his gaze and saw his steely determination. "I swear!"

With a horrible sense of foreboding, she ran. Behind her, Harte fired three quick shots, covering her.

"Harte, run!" she cried. She reached the building and ducked behind it, pressing her back against the wall. If she angled her head, she could see Harte.

He was inching up from behind the tires to check the shooter's position. When he did, a shot rang out, but to Dani's surprise, it ricocheted off the wall close to her head, sending shards of plaster flying. She ducked back.

"Bastard," she heard Harte growl; then he vaulted up and ran, firing rapidly.

Dani backed up as Harte rounded the corner of the building and slammed back against the wall. "You okay?" he panted.

"Yes."

"I know where we are. Through this alley is Tchoupitoulas Street," he said, pressing the back of his head against the wall and angling around to fire off another couple of rounds, then ducking back. "Did you see the words painted on this building? This is the back of La Maisson Restaurant. La Maisson fronts onto Tchoupitoulas and it's only about three blocks from my great-aunt Claire's house."

Gunshots peppered the corner where he'd just leaned out.

"Go through there. At the end of the alley, go left. Don't look back. I'll catch up." He leaned out and fired again.

Dani ran as fast as she could, her sneakers squeaking on the asphalt. She heard footsteps behind her and prayed it was Harte and not one of the goons who were trying to kill them.

The air was filled with gunfire. Her neck prickled, her scalp burned and her lungs felt strained to the point of bursting, but she didn't dare stop.

She heard a short, pained groan behind her and the footsteps stumbled unevenly. She dared a glance backward in time to see Harte regain his footing. "Harte—" she gasped.

"Don't stop!" he shouted.

Sirens suddenly wailed behind them, and then Harte caught up with her. He passed her, pointing at a blue building. "Through that alley," he shouted, and slowed down. "Go!"

She ran past him and into the alley, but she had no idea which way to turn out the other end, so she slowed to a stop.

The siren changed to short blasts. Maybe they'd caught the men.

Harte ran around the corner a few seconds later. He leaned against the wall, his chest heaving and sweat dripping in rivulets down his face. "Aunt Claire's house is right behind here. White with green shutters. Come on."

Dani frowned at him. Something was wrong. "Harte—?"

"Move! No time to talk." He took off down the alley and she followed.

Then she saw it—the blood on his shirt. "You're bleeding!" she cried.

He didn't acknowledge her. He just kept on across the street, dodging tree limbs and trash and torn roofing shingles, then bounded up a set of stone steps to ornate double doors with stained-glass sidelights and transom.

He turned the handle and pushed against the door, but it didn't open. He hammered on the wood with the gun. "Paul!" he cried in a strained voice. "Open up! It's Harte."

Chapter Fourteen

Harte pounded on the door again. "Paul!"

Before the word was out of his mouth, the door flew open and Harte's cousin on his grandmother Lilibelle's side, Paul Guillame, stood there, surprise and anger on his face. "Harte? What the—? Do you know what time it is?"

Harte pushed past Paul with Dani in tow. Paul's strident voice penetrated the haze in his brain. "Good Lord! You're bleeding! Is that a gun?"

"He's been shot," Dani cried. "We need to get him to a doctor."

Paul sent her a quizzical look, then turned back to Harte. "Who is this? And what's going on?"

Despite the seriousness of the situation, despite the bullet wound that hurt like hell, Harte shook his head at Paul's blithering. But the black at the edges of his vision was growing and he knew he'd pass out if he didn't sit or lie down. "Shut the door, Paul. We've got dangerous men after us."

Paul's black eyes widened, showing white all the way around the irises. "Dangerous men?" He craned his neck around the door, then pushed it closed and locked it with shaking hands. "Why did you come here?"

While Paul was talking, Harte felt Dani's hand on his good arm. She pulled him through the foyer and into the large, too-warm front room. A fire was blazing in the large fireplace. He was already feeling light-headed from loss of blood. The heat made him feel as though he couldn't get a breath. He stopped for a moment, leaning against the faux-finished walls of his aunt Claire's house, trying not to pass out.

"Not in there!" Paul cried, hurrying toward them as Dani guided Harte toward an ornately carved sofa upholstered in ivory. "Take him to the kitchen. Through there." He gestured in a shooing motion. "Put him in one of the kitchen chairs."

Harte let Dani guide him through open French doors that separated the living room and dining room and on past the huge mahogany dining table into the dark kitchen. He sank into a chair with a pained sigh. His pulse was racing and he thought he could feel blood pouring out of his wound. There was a towel on the counter and he got his feet under him and reached for it, but Dani put her hand on his chest and pushed him back into the chair.

"You sit right there," she ordered him. "And give me that!" She took the SIG out of his hand, thumbed the safety on and shoved it into her purse.

She straightened and turned to Paul, who had grabbed a candelabra in his hand—a real silver candelabra sporting eight blazing tapers. "Where's your phone?" she demanded.

Paul set the candelabra in the middle of the wooden kitchen table. "Does it look like we have any of the conveniences?"

Harte squeezed his eyes shut, trying to get rid of the odd haze that was enveloping his brain. He dug out his phone and flipped it open. "Still no bars," he said, hearing the strain in his voice. "And I'm about out of battery too."

Dani had sat down next to him and was trying to pull the material of his shirt away from the bullet wound in his upper chest. "I need a first-aid kit," she commanded.

Paul gestured vaguely with his right hand. "It's up there—in the cabinet above the sink," he said.

"Get it, please," she said archly. "Hot water too, and cloths."

Harte winced as another square inch of material tore away from the dried blood at the edge of his wound. He could barely swallow. He needed fluids. Blinking against the haze that seemed to be growing denser every second, he saw that Paul held a highball glass in his hand. "Hand me that drink," he said.

"This is my Pimm's and lemonade," Paul said, glancing at Harte, then at Dani. "That's the last of the ice." With a shrug, he handed it to Harte.

The glass was about half-full and dripping with condensation. There were three tiny, melting ice cubes floating in it. When Harte wrapped his fingers around it, a chill slid through him. He turned it up and drank. The cool liquid burned his throat as rivulets of water dripped down his chin and neck. He shivered.

By the time he'd drained the glass and wiped his face with his wet hand, Paul had set a plastic box and a couple of kitchen towels on the table and was running water into a bowl. Dani grabbed scissors from the first-aid kit and started cutting Harte's shirtsleeve off. "He needs more water," she said.

Paul picked up the glass and went to the sink.

"Just wrap it—stop the bleeding," Harte protested. "Paul, give me your car keys. We've got to get to a police station."

"Harte, for crying out loud," Paul snapped as he set the glass down in front of Harte. "Don't you think if I could move my car we'd be in Biloxi—or Jackson—right now?"

"Why can't you?" he asked.

"A branch fell right across the driveway."

Harte took a drink of water. "How big is it?"

"It doesn't matter," Dani snapped. "*You* won't be moving it." She dipped a towel in the tepid water, then laid it like a compress over his wound. The little bit of heat felt wonderful and awful at the same time. He groaned.

Dani spoke as she pressed the compress tightly against his shoulder. "So, how big is the branch?" she asked Paul. "Could you and I move it?"

Paul's eyes widened. "Certainly not. It's huge—more of a tree than a branch."

At that instant, Harte saw movement in the dim candlelight of the dining room. "Who's there?" he demanded. Asking the question seemed to use up all his air.

Dani shot up from her chair and pulled the gun out of her purse. He heard the safety click.

"What are you doing?" Paul cried. "Put that gun away. Myron, you might as well come out. Harte, you've met Senator Stamps," he said. "We were having a business discussion over dinner when the storm hit."

Myron Stamps stepped out of the shadows and into the flickering circle of candlelight.

"Stamps?" Harte almost laughed at the irony. "Where's your car?"

Senator Stamps shrugged. "Behind Paul's in his driveway. You wouldn't get very far, even if you had a car," he said. "There are trees and billboards and who knows what other debris all over the streets. It's awful. Our city isn't ready for more destruction and tragedy."

Dani was wrapping gauze around a makeshift compress she'd placed against the wound in Harte's shoulder. She paused and turned to look at the senator.

"Really?" she said archly as she ripped the gauze off the roll. "You're practicing sound bites for a new campaign already?"

"Young woman," Paul said. "I don't know who you are, but you are out of line—"

Dani broke in. "You don't know who I am?"

Harte grunted as she tied the loose ends of the gauze.

She stood. "Well, let me introduce myself. I'm Danielle Canto. I know *he* knows me," she added, indicating Stamps.

Paul turned his gaze full on her for the first time. "Oh," he said. "You're Freeman Canto's granddaughter?" He took a pair of glasses from the pocket of his lounging jacket and peered through them without putting them on. "Oh yes, I recognize you now." He turned to Harte. "I'd heard you were handling Freeman Canto's murder, but, Harte, what has this person gotten you into?"

"Hey!" Dani took two steps to plant her feet directly in front of him. She stared up at him, her chin thrust out. "How dare you! I'm the person who heard my grandfather's murderers threaten him using your name—" She pointed a finger at him, then at Stamps. "And yours."

"Dani!" Harte cried, forcing himself to his feet and grabbing her arm as his cousin's face went deathly pale and Stamps made a growling sound deep in his throat. He knew why she was so upset, and he couldn't blame her, but he had no idea what Paul or Stamps would do, and he was too weak to defend her if her accusations made them violent.

Dani whirled.

Paul cried, "Oh—no, no, no. I had nothing to do with all that. It was all between Yeoman and Myr—"

"Shut up!" Stamps yelled, lunging at Paul.

Paul screeched and hopped aside as Stamps, with too much forward motion to check himself, barreled into Harte, then stumbled over him and plowed into the side of the stainless-steel refrigerator.

Harte fell on his left shoulder. He felt gauze and tape tear. Blood, hot and wet, immediately soaked the bandage. Cold sweat popped out on his forehead and trickled down into his eyes. He blindly struggled up into a crouch, but nausea enveloped him and he wasn't sure he could stay upright. As the red haze of pain faded from his eyes, a black halo started closing in around the edges of his vision.

Just then a deafening crash thundered through the house. Paul yelped as the front door shattered.

Men spilled through the opening, kicking splinters and planks of wood aside. The flickering light from the candles and the fire reflected redly off the metal of their guns.

A deep voice shouted, "You! Go around!"

"Dani, watch out!" Harte yelled. He grabbed the edge of the kitchen table and tried to lift it. Dani immediately saw what he was doing and ran to help him. The two of them upended the table with a bang. He crouched behind it. Dani threw herself down beside him.

"What's going on?" Paul cried from behind the corner wall that opened onto the dining room. "Do something!"

Out of the corner of his eye, Harte saw Stamps open the refrigerator door and hide behind it. Beside Harte, Dani pulled out her gun.

"Give it to me," he said.

Dani gave Harte a sidelong glance. He was pale and his lips were pinched and white at the corners. He looked as if he would pass out any second. "Not a chance," she snapped. "You're wounded. Switch sides with me."

"Dani—"

"Do it!" she hissed, and crawled behind him. "Move, Harte! I mean it. And stay down."

She saw the irritation and resignation in his eyes as he acquiesced. It hurt him that she wouldn't let him protect her, she knew, but she didn't have time to argue or persuade. He was wounded and too weak to handle the gun, and she had to be able to aim and shoot with her right hand.

She clicked off the safety and sat up and held her gun in her right hand, steadied by her left. Carefully, she eased her head up enough to get a glimpse of the men. She needed to see their positions and, if possible, get a look at their armament.

There were two of them casting about blindly, working to get their bearings in the dark living room after being outside in the brightness of the rising sun. The one on the left was the brute who'd grabbed her. She could tell by his size and the tan raincoat. She aimed low and fired. He yelped and went down.

She ducked back behind the table.

"Paul!" Harte yelled. "Get out the back and go for help!"

"What?" Paul's mouth fell open. "Me?"

"Hurry!" Dani snapped. "One of them is going around the back."

"I can't!" Paul gasped.

"Watch out," Dani cried. "Duck!"

Sure enough, a firestorm of bullets peppered the walls, the tabletop and the stainless-steel refrigerator.

Paul cowered farther into the corner. With a moue of disgust for the man, she popped up again and fired off four quick bursts.

"Damn," she whispered. She could tell from the weight of the weapon that the magazine was almost empty. Why hadn't she counted how many times Harte had fired it? She slung her purse off over her head. "Get my other clip!" she told Harte.

She fired again, and again the men responded with a burst of pistol fire. As the noise from the explosions faded, she thought she heard police sirens. She exchanged a quick glance with Harte.

He handed her the fresh clip. When she took it, she felt the sticky slickness of blood on it.

Harte's blood. Her pulse pounded in her throat as she ejected the nearly empty magazine and inserted the new one, then braced herself to rise and fire again. If she didn't keep up a barrage of bullets, the men would rush them and kill them. She'd hit the brute who'd grabbed her the night before, but she wasn't sure she'd hurt him.

She glanced behind her. Paul was still tucked into the corner and Stamps was still behind the refrigerator door. She didn't see a back door. She'd just have to deal with the third guy when he showed up.

As she turned back to shoot another round at the men in front of them, a gun fired behind her. She jerked in surprise. Before she could distinguish where exactly the shot had come from, Paul let out a tortured cry and fell to the floor.

She turned her head, preparing to whirl and take out the shooter, but Harte yelled, "Got him!"

"No! Harte!" she cried, but it was too late. He had vaulted up. She heard a thud and two grunts and knew he'd connected with the shooter.

Don't you dare get killed after all we've been through, she thought desperately as one of the men in front of them angled around the French doors and fired directly at her. She ducked behind the table, heard the bullet zing past her ear, then rose and shot several rounds at the open doors.

A startled cry told her that one of her bullets had found its mark. Suddenly, the staccato yelp of police sirens sounded, deafeningly loud, and a bullhorn roared.

They heard a voice, accompanied by more short bursts of the siren. "Police! Drop your weapons! Drop them! Now!"

Dani rose slowly, her gun at the ready, and pointed toward the two men. The man in the tan raincoat, the goon who had grabbed her in the alley, was on his knees. He dropped his weapon and leaned a hand against the wall. His pant leg was soaked with blood.

The second man stood, feet splayed apart, his gun aimed directly at her. Blood dripped from his left hand. She straightened, her barrel pointed right at the space between his eyes.

"Drop it," she growled, just as two uniformed policemen appeared at the front door.

"Drop it!" they shouted in unison. "Now!" One officer advanced as the other continued to shout.

"Drop it and hit the floor," the advancing officer yelled. "Do it or I'll shoot."

The first officer stepped past the brute and kicked his gun at least four feet across the living room floor. He stopped just out of arm's reach of the man who was still aiming at Dani. "Drop it or you're a dead man," he said.

The shooter jerked, startled that the officer was so close to him. He let the gun dangle by the handle from his hand. The officer grabbed his arm. The gun hit the floor and the officer slammed the man against the wall and cuffed him.

Dani gasped for air. Had she been holding her breath or had fear sucked all the oxygen from her lungs?

At that instant, a tall man with blazing blue eyes and an NOPD badge pinned to the waistband of his jeans stepped into the room, breathing hard. "Where's Harte?" he demanded.

Dani was wondering the same thing. She turned

around and what she saw shocked her. Harte was on the floor, holding someone in a half nelson. That someone was grunting and snuffling like a pig headed to slaughter. To her surprise, she realized it was Myron Stamps.

"Lucas," Harte wheezed as he let go of Stamps. His pale face and labored breathing told her there was something terribly wrong.

The detective stepped past Paul, who was writhing on the floor whimpering, and grabbed hold of Stamps's collar.

"Gun!" Harte rasped.

The detective dropped the man like a hot potato and put his foot on his neck. "Don't move," he barked. Bending, he wrenched the gun from Stamps's hand.

As he cuffed the senator, he glanced at Harte. "How you doing, kid?" he said.

"He's shot," Dani cried. "He's bleeding." She crawled toward him on her knees.

From the corner of the kitchen came a whining voice. "Lucas, help me. I'm shot too," Paul squealed. "I think it's serious."

Lucas. The detective was Harte's older brother. "How'd you find us?" she asked.

Lucas knelt next to Harte. "Got your messages and went to the drugstore. Then I heard gunshots. I called for the closest police cruiser."

"Thank goodness you got here," Dani said as more sirens filled the air.

Lucas jerked his head in the direction of the sound. "That's the EMTs," he said shortly. "I was afraid they wouldn't be able to get through. Kid? How'd you get yourself shot?"

"I'm okay," Harte said weakly, lifting his head. "Just my shoulder."

Dani crawled over to him and cradled his head. "It's not his shoulder. It's his chest. See?" She showed Lucas the bandage. "He's lost so much blood."

Harte shook his head. Then it hit her. Lucas was his oldest brother. He was the one Harte had told her gave him such a hard time for becoming a prosecutor instead of a cop. Harte didn't want to look weak in front of him.

No danger of that, she thought. He'd taken care of her, saved her more times than she could count and fought off the men who were trying to capture her or, worse, kill her. Even after taking a bullet in the chest, he'd still fought to keep her safe.

She looked up at Lucas, who met her gaze. She saw in his expressive face that he was thinking the same thing. Then he leaned over his younger brother. "Somebody get those EMTs in here now! My brother's been shot."

Harte lifted his head. "Paul's wounded," he gasped, "and Dani took down at least one of the shooters."

"Yeah," Lucas said, frowning. Then he added louder, "Get the damned EMTs!"

Chapter Fifteen

Dani wanted to go to the hospital with Harte, but the police had a different idea. After she was examined and released by the EMTs, she was taken to the police station, where she spent all the rest of the morning and a large part of the afternoon being questioned and writing out and signing her statement. Someone had found her a clean set of scrubs and a blanket to wrap up in, but she still had on her wet sneakers.

She glanced at the clock over the door for what had to be the two hundredth time. It had been over an hour since anyone had even peeked in to see if the room was free. Had they forgotten about her?

She picked up the foam cup that held what might have passed for coffee two hours ago, but was now sludge. One whiff and she set it down and pushed it as far away as she could.

At that instant the doorknob turned. It was Lucas. He had her purse in tow. "I gotta say this is the biggest purse I've ever seen."

"Thank God you're here," Dani said. "I can go now, right? I need to see Harte. How is he?"

"He'll be fine," Lucas said. "I've got an officer waiting to drive you to a hotel."

"You mean to my house."

"No," he said evenly. "I mean to the hotel. You're still under an order of protection until the trial is over, and it's been delayed."

"Delayed?" She wanted to cry. She was exhausted and filthy and sleepy and hungry. The pallid vending-machine ham sandwich and watery soda she'd had who knew how many hours ago were long gone.

Lucas nodded. "The D.A. is assigning another prosecutor to handle the trial, and he or she will need time to get up to speed."

"Why another prosecutor? You told me Harte was going to be fine." She grabbed Lucas's arm. "Please. Is he okay?"

Lucas narrowed his eyes. "He *is* going to be fine. They're giving him blood. As soon as they can, they'll get him into surgery. Apparently, the bullet hit the top of his left lung."

"Oh no," she said. That was why he'd sounded wheezy, why he'd struggled so much to take a breath. "But they can get it out. Just go in and—" she put her thumb and forefinger together "—pluck it out. Right?"

Lucas looked somber. "They think so. It's pretty close to his heart."

"Close to—?" Her pulse pounded in her throat. "Have you seen him? Talked to him?"

"They've got him sedated. They don't want that bullet to move."

"Oh," she moaned, sinking into a chair. She pressed her palm against her chest. Her heart felt as though it was going to burst wide open, it was hurting that much. "I didn't know how bad he was hurt."

"Hey," Lucas said, rubbing his forehead. "The doctors know what they're doing."

His tone didn't match his reassuring words. She looked up at him. He looked exhausted. His hair was furrowed and sticking up as if he'd run his fingers through it multiple times. He had a smudge of dirt on his cheek and a scrape on the knuckles of his left hand. But what frightened Dani was the look on his face. His brow was furrowed and his mouth was grim.

"You're worried," she said.

He met her gaze. His mouth curved upward slightly, in a duplicate of Harte's crooked smile. The sight of it made her heart ache.

"I am," he said, "but Harte is tough and stubborn. A little thing like a bullet won't stop him. It wouldn't dare."

Dani smiled back at him, even though her eyes were burning. "You're right about that. He is pretty stubborn," she said.

"He comes by that naturally."

She studied him for a brief moment. "You and he don't look much alike. I mean obviously you do, but—"

"That's because he took after the French side of the family, and I got the Irish genes." As he spoke, he opened the interrogation room door for her, then closed it behind them. A young uniformed officer was waiting outside the room.

"Dani Canto, this is Officer Roebuck. He'll take you to the hotel."

The officer nodded. She acknowledged him with a brief nod of her head. "Officer, will you be my dayshift babysitter?"

"No," Lucas said. "You won't have a guard during the day. Just at night."

"So I'm in less danger than I was?" Dani shook her head. "How exactly does that work?"

"The men who chased you are in custody, for one thing."

Dani pushed her tangled hair back from her face. "Good," she said tiredly. "So, Officer Roebuck, shall we go?"

"Yes, ma'am," Roebuck said. "The car's out front." He stood back to let her precede him.

Dani turned back to Lucas. "Can we swing by the hospital to see Harte?"

Lucas shook his head.

"Lucas—Detective, I need to see him." She bit her lip, doing her best to look him in the eye, to appear strong and capable, not small and scared that she might never see Harte again.

"I told you, he's sedated. They're not letting anybody see him right now." Lucas looked past her at Roebuck and nodded.

"Ma'am?" Roebuck said. "We need to get going."

Dani couldn't tear her gaze away from Lucas. "Please don't lie to me," she said. "It's too important."

He glanced at Officer Roebuck and nodded toward the door. The officer walked toward the exit door to wait. Once he was out of hearing, Lucas stepped close to her.

"Harte is unconscious. They're taking him to surgery any minute now. It's going to be touch-and-go. If the bullet shifts, it could go into his heart. My parents are there with my sister, waiting."

Dani pressed her lips together, working to stay calm. Her heart was threatening to burst again. She could barely breathe, her throat was so tight. But she heard Lucas loud and clear.

Harte is in critical condition. He needs his family.

"I understand," she said hoarsely, then grabbed his shirtsleeve. "Please, when you can, have someone call me?"

"Okay," he said gently. "As soon as I can." He turned and walked toward another detective who was obviously waiting to talk to him. She saw him rub the back of his neck as he spoke to the other man.

Dani squeezed her eyes shut. She couldn't wipe away the vision of Harte's soft, dark gaze as he'd lowered his head to kiss her, or the pinched pallor of his face as he'd looked up at his big brother and tried to pretend he wasn't bleeding to death.

They'd been on the run together for less than twelve hours. But she didn't think she could live if he died.

ETHAN DELANCEY DIDN'T like hospitals. People died there. He paced back and forth between the window and the door of the private room where his youngest brother lay—too quiet, too pale, too still.

He stopped and looked at Harte for what must have been the twentieth time. How the hell had this happened? He and Lucas and Travis were the ones who flirted with danger. It was cops and soldiers who took their lives in their hands, who went out there day after day to try to make the world a safer place. They understood the risk. They dealt with it.

Harte hadn't followed in his brothers' footsteps. He'd

taken a different path—the path of their dad and their notorious grandfather. He was a *lawyer*. Lawyers didn't get shot.

Ethan walked over to the bed. He felt so damn helpless. Reaching out, he straightened the tubes that fed oxygen through Harte's nostrils. Then he brushed thick dark hair off his brother's forehead.

Behind him, he heard the room door open. He turned. It was Lucas. "Hey," he said.

"How is he?" Lucas asked, closing the door and coming up beside Ethan.

Ethan shook his head. "No change. Didn't the doctor say he'd be awake by now? It's been almost twenty-four hours since the surgery."

Lucas nodded. "The surgeon said they wanted him to sleep as much as possible. That's why they kept him in the ICU for twelve hours."

Ethan rubbed his temples and flopped down in a hard vinyl chair near the bed. Lucas leaned against the wall near the window. He crossed his arms.

"You look pretty scruffy," Ethan observed. "What's the latest?"

Lucas sighed and rubbed his jaw, his palm scraping like sandpaper across the stubble. "When did I talk to you last?"

"Yesterday, after you got Dani to the hotel."

"You mean Saturday."

"No, I mean yesterday. You'd talked to Paul, but you said Stamps had lawyered up."

"Right. After I got Paul's statement that it was Stamps who'd shot him, I talked to Stamps's lawyer. That was a massive waste of time. She claimed he was sedated after the traumatic events and couldn't be questioned."

Ethan laughed. "Seriously?"

"I'm thinking she's setting him up for an insanity defense."

"What about Paul?"

"I asked her what their response to his accusation would be, and she wouldn't talk about it." Lucas shook his head. "I'm trying to get a court order to test for gunshot residue—"

"Talk about a waste of time," Ethan put in.

"I know. Stamps, sedated or not, will have hosed himself down by then."

"What do you think about Paul saying Stamps shot him?"

"That's odd too. Paul was nearly hysterical at the scene, screaming that Stamps had tried to kill him. I've got several witnesses that heard him. But later, after he was discharged from the emergency room, he said it was an accident. Said Stamps was firing wildly." Lucas sat on the small couch under the window and leaned forward, elbows on knees.

"I thought you told me—"

"That Stamps only fired one shot?" He nodded. "That's right. I did."

"And you've got the gun," Ethan said, glancing over at Harte's pale face. "A senior senator shooting people, our distant cousin somehow involved—what the hell did the kid dig up?"

"Well, he was right about one thing. Ernest Yeoman is in it up to his neck. And he's not going to walk this time."

"The D.A.'s probably over the moon. So the no-necks Dani shot are Yeoman's men?"

Lucas nodded smugly. "They weren't carrying any ID, but here's a shocker. They were both in the system."

"Yeah? Who were they?"

"Couple of small-time crooks. You know how it goes." Lucas pulled a small notebook out of his pocket. He flipped a few pages. "One of them was Chester Kirkle, the guy who left the fingerprint on Canto's office door the night he was killed," he said.

"Right. Harte was hoping to cut a deal with him. I thought he was remanded."

"Somehow, this past week, he got himself a decent lawyer and made bail. No information where he got the money." Lucas rubbed the back of his neck.

"Do you think he's still willing to cut the deal?"

"Oh yeah. I dangled aggravated assault three over his head."

That surprised Ethan. "A. A. Three? Can you make that stick?"

"Hell yeah," Lucas said, gesturing at Harte. "The D.A. authorized it. They wounded a public official with a deadly weapon, threatened a second and were fleeing from law enforcement. And one or more of them may have been involved in the murder of Freeman Canto."

Ethan smiled. That was what made Lucas one of the best detectives on the force. Better even than Dixon Lloyd, Ethan's partner. He gave Lucas a tip of an imaginary hat. "Good job. What'd they cough up?"

"Get this. Kirkle's playing the deal card. Says he had Harte's promise of a deal if he talked, so now he's singing about Yeoman. He claims Yeoman sent them to *persuade* Canto to reverse his position on tariffs and one of the goons got too rough."

"What do you think?"

"I'm inclined to believe him. If he rolls on Yeoman, the D.A. and a lot of other people will be ecstatic."

Ethan looked at Harte again. "One of them shot Harte," he said, hearing the catch in his voice.

Lucas heard it too, because he sent him a sharp glance, then stood and walked over to the bed. He touched Harte's hand where the IV tubing snaked out from a white bandage with a tiny spot of blood on it. "I know," he said. "I'd like to bury both of them, but they're punks. Nobodies. We need to get Yeoman if we can."

Ethan didn't say anything. He and Lucas stared at their baby brother for a moment. Finally, Lucas patted Harte's hand and turned toward the door. "I've got to go. I'm going to run home and shower, then—"

"Good," Ethan interrupted. "It's about time."

Lucas shot him a warning look. "Then I'm heading over to Impound. The vehicle is a Lincoln Town Car and it's totaled."

"They used it to break down a freight door at that warehouse where Harte and Dani were hiding, right?"

Lucas nodded.

Ethan shook his head. "I can't wait for Harte to tell us how he managed to keep away from them all night long."

"I know. So the crime scene guys collected paint and glass fragments from the vehicle that rammed the warehouse freight door and ran them. They matched the glass and paint the car left at the scene at Dani's house."

"They used the same car? That's amazing."

"You want amazing, guess who owns the car."

"Not Yeoman—" Ethan said.

"It's registered to the general manager of the Hasty Mart Corporation."

Ethan was stunned. "Are you kidding me? Yeoman's got to be smarter than that. Otherwise, how has he managed to stay out of jail all this time?"

"I don't know," Lucas said, rubbing a hand down his face. "Maybe it was his henchmen who were too dumb to change vehicles. All I can say is thank God for stupid crooks."

Ethan laughed. "Way to go. That plus Dani's testimony should nail the SOB."

"It should." Lucas sighed. He looked at his watch. "What are you doing the rest of the afternoon? Is Mom coming over?"

"She said she might be here around six, after she fixes dinner for Dad." Ethan stood and stretched. "I think I'll stay here until she gets here. I've got a feeling the kid might wake up soon."

"All right, E. Call me if he does, okay? And try to get some rest."

Ethan nodded and held out his hand. Lucas took it and the two shared a quick, awkward man-hug.

Once Lucas was gone, Ethan thought about turning on the TV, but he wasn't in the mood for seven million channels and nothing on. So he yawned, then sat back and closed his eyes.

Rest sounded good. He had been up all night sitting with Harte, and was exhausted. Lucas, on the other hand, had worked the crime scene, and was about to head back out for a third shift with no rest.

Lucas had always been a superhero in Ethan's eyes.

Chapter Sixteen

Harte's whole body hurt worse with every move he made. They'd been running for so long that he and Dani were both exhausted. He glanced back to check on Dani, but suddenly, darkness enveloped everything.

"Dani?" he cried, but she didn't answer. "Dani, answer me."

Nothing.

"Dani!" She was gone. His biggest fear had come to pass. He'd failed to keep her safe.

"Hey, kid? Wake up."

Harte heard someone. Was it Dani? God, he hoped so. But the voice sounded far away. Indistinct.

"Harte? Are you trying to wake up?"

The voice beckoned him. But the closer he got to it, the more he hurt. Who was trying to keep him from finding Dani?

"Leave me alone. I've got to find Dani."

"Harte, it's Ethan. Talk to me, kid."

Ethan? Harte felt as though the bottom had dropped out from under him. He opened his eyes to slits, which made his head hurt. Everything was an ugly, dull blue color.

"Ethan?" he rasped as his brain slowly began to process what his senses were taking in. A small TV on a stand was suspended from the ceiling in front of him. Under it, a whiteboard held a sign in big letters that read Today is_____. There was nothing written in the blank. His nostrils burned with the mingled smells of disinfectant and rubbing alcohol, and he could hear a continuous hiss-pop, hiss-pop.

From somewhere, a different voice spoke. "Everything all right? Does Mr. Delancey need ice water or towels?"

"No, thanks."

Then everything coalesced in his brain. His eyes flew open wide. "Oh no," he moaned. "Not the hospital."

His brother Ethan's face moved into his field of vision. "Can't understand a word you're saying," he said, smiling. "Want some water?"

Water sounded wonderful. Harte licked his lips, or tried to. They were so dry they barely moved.

Ethan held a big cup and guided the plastic straw into Harte's mouth. When the first splash of cold water hit his tongue, the chill shot all the way through him. He shuddered, then greedily sucked up more.

"Whoa," Ethan said, taking the cup away. "The nurse said you could have a *little*."

His lips still felt parched, but inside, he was feeling much better. He tried to push himself upright, but that turned out to be a bad idea.

"Ahhh!" he growled, and collapsed back into the soft bedclothes. He muttered a few choice curses, which actually seemed to help.

"Nice," Ethan said, pulling a chair up beside the bed. "Good thing Mom's not here."

Harte growled again. "Am I in a hospital?" he asked, trying his best to control his thick tongue.

"Okay. What I think I heard is *hospital*. So yes, you're in the hospital."

Harte's eyes were still burning, so he closed them. "What am I doing here?"

"Good. You're getting better. You and Dani Canto were attacked at the B-and-B, so you ran and hid all night through that mother of a storm. Somewhere in there you got shot. Then you ended up at Paul's house with the bad guys on your tail. Paul took a bullet and a couple of your pursuers were shot. The cavalry arrived and saved the day. You had surgery and voilà, here you are."

"Not quite all that happened," Harte muttered between gritted teeth. "Where's Dani? Is she all right?"

Ethan nodded, his expression turning more serious. "She's fine. The EMTs examined her at the scene and released her. You, on the other hand, have a great big surgery to recuperate from. By the way, the nurse also told me you'd be too drowsy to make sense." Ethan's frown faded. "I see she was right about that."

"I'm fine," Harte muttered. The nurse was correct. He could barely hold his eyes open and he had to concentrate like mad to keep up with what Ethan was saying. But there was no way he was going to let his older brother know that.

"Fine," he repeated, looking out the window. He couldn't see anything but sky and the top of a portion of the New Orleans skyline. He didn't even try to figure out what direction the window faced. "What time is it?"

"Six-twenty."

He stared at his brother, then blinked and gave his head a shake. "Six-twenty?"

Ethan's mouth turned up. "Twenty minutes after six."

"P.m.?" He reached up to rub his forehead, where the groggy haze seemed centered, and discovered that his hand had an IV hooked up to it. He growled.

"Here," Ethan said, picking up the cup again. "Drink some more water before you fall asleep."

This time, he reached for the cup, but the IV tubing that was inserted in his hand got caught in the bed-clothes. Ethan untangled it and handed him the cup.

Harte sipped slowly. His stomach didn't feel great, but the water—a little water—helped. "Thanks," he said.

Ethan took the cup from his hand and set it down on the rolling table. "You're going to fall asleep and spill that all over yourself."

"Six-twenty," Harte said thoughtfully. "I've been here all day? When can we leave?"

Ethan shook his head indulgently. "Not so fast, kid. You haven't been here all day. You've been here since Saturday morning. Today's Sunday."

Harte stared at him in horror. "Sunday? What happened to Saturday?"

"You spent a lot of Saturday unconscious. They sedated you so they could give you blood. Then they took you into surgery. The doctor said you wouldn't remember anything, and I guess he's right."

"What about—the—trial?" Harte was having a lot of trouble staying awake.

"The trial's been set to start Thursday."

"Okay. I can be—ready by Thursday."

Ethan laughed. "Oh, trust me, kid. You will not be ready by Thursday. The D.A. has got another prosecutor working twenty-four-seven to get up to speed."

"What?" Harte tried to sit up, but couldn't. "My case!"

"Hey," Ethan said, patting the sheet near Harte's hand. "You don't need to worry about the trial. You just need to rest and get better." He stood. "I'm going to go tell the nurses that you're awake, then I'll head out. Mom will probably be over later to see you."

"Wait," Harte said. "Where's Dani? She been here?"

"Nope. She's in protective custody, remember? She's not allowed to go anywhere."

"I want to see her. Make sure she's all right." Harte tried to sit up. He put most of his weight on his right arm. With a lot of effort and a lot of pain, he managed to scoot a little more upright in the bed.

"Hang on," Ethan said with an exaggerated sigh. "You're going to rip out all of the doctor's pretty stitching." He leaned over and pressed a button on the console that hung from the bed rail. The head of the bed rose, pushing Harte into a more upright, seated position.

"Thanks," he said. "I need to see Dani."

"She's just fine. If you're going to be stubborn, I'll call the head nurse. I think she was a drill sergeant."

"Call her."

"Harte, you haven't seen this nurse—at least not that you remember."

As if she were summoned by Ethan's threat, the door to Harte's room opened and a large, imposing woman in white slacks and an incongruous lavender scrub shirt with pink puppies and kittens on it entered. She had an IV bag in her sizeable hands.

"Mr. Delancey, you're awake." The nurse leveled a glare at Ethan, then the badge pinned to his jacket pocket. "And *you* are still here." Stepping around the bed and past Ethan, she replaced the nearly empty IV bag with the new one and adjusted the flow.

Then she inspected the IV cannula in Harte's hand, walked around to the other side of the bed and looked at the large bandage that covered from just beneath the collarbone to his upper abdomen. Then she lifted her head and peered through the lower half of her glasses at the LED screen of the heart monitor mounted above the bed.

"How are you feeling?" she asked, her voice gentler than her physical presence might suggest. "Having any pain?"

He gave a halfhearted right-shoulder shrug. "I'm okay," he said.

She looked up at Ethan. "I'm going to give him a dose of morphine. I'd suggest you go interrogate somebody who's up and around." When she glanced back at Harte, he saw a fleeting glint of amusement in her eyes. "My patient here needs to rest."

"Yes, ma'am," Ethan said, rolling his eyes in Harte's direction. "I'll be back later, kid." He stood, leaned over and planted a kiss on the top of Harte's head, sent a quelling look at the nurse when she grinned at his sentimental gesture and left.

"There you go," the nurse said as she pressed a button on the IV flow meter of a second bag that was piggybacked into the first. "A nice little boost of morphine."

"Not too much," Harte murmured. He could already feel the drug doing its job.

"You aren't getting too much. You're getting just the right amount. You'd better sleep while you can. Tomorrow morning, your nurse is going to make you get up and walk."

"How soon can I get out of here?" he asked.

"I'll let you and the doctor talk about that." She nodded toward the door. "So, I suppose that was your brother? Nice guy. You and he must be close. You look like twins."

"He wishes he was as good-looking as me," Harte muttered, unable to keep his eyes open any longer. He heard the nurse chuckle as she went out of the room.

Chapter Seventeen

Dani sat in the courtroom, waiting for the judge and jury to enter. The jury had reported about an hour ago that they had reached a verdict.

The judge entered and, in doing so, stopped the idle chatter in the courtroom. He stepped up behind the bench and spoke to the prosecution's attorneys and then to the defense's, ensuring that they were ready to proceed.

"Bailiff, you may bring in the jury," the judge said.

"Your Honor?" asked Natalie Shallowford, the attorney the D.A. had assigned to take over for Harte. "May I approach?"

The judge nodded and so she did so, along with Felix Drury, the defense attorney. After a short, quiet conversation, the judge nodded and the two attorneys returned to their seats.

Dani heard the door to the courtroom open and saw the judge nod to whoever had come in. Most of the observers turned around, then started murmuring.

The judge pounded his gavel. "Quiet!" he demanded. "Welcome back, Mr. Delancey."

Dani's heart pounded. She half turned, but because she was just behind the prosecution's table, she couldn't

see at first. Then she heard footsteps and a slight metallic creaking sound.

Natalie Shallowford opened the gate and a court officer wheeled Harte Delancey, in a wheelchair, through
the gate and over to the prosecution's table.

Dani looked at him for the first time since he'd been
taken away by ambulance almost a week ago. He was
pale and drawn, and his eyes had circles under them.
His arm was in a dark blue sling. Her heart squeezed
with compassion. He'd come very close to dying, she
knew. Lucas had told her it had been a long surgery to
remove the bullet that had clipped the upper edge of
his lung, near his heart.

Once the bullet was out, Lucas had told her, everything was fine and he would recover quickly. But he
didn't look recovered yet. She wasn't sure why Lucas
had let him come to court. It would be exhausting for
him.

The jury came in and the judge quickly ran through
their duties and responsibilities. Then, finally, he asked
for the verdict.

The foreman stood. "As to count one, murder in the
first degree, we the jury find the defendant, Ernest W.
Yeoman—not guilty."

Dani's heart sank. *Not guilty.* She'd expected it, but
the two words still cut like a knife.

Ernest Yeoman, standing behind the defense table,
pumped a fist in the air. Felix Drury, his powerhouse attorney, laid a subtle hand on his arm. Yeoman straightened as the foreman continued.

"As to the second count, conspiracy to commit murder—"

Dani braced herself. Based on the way the trial had gone, she figured aggravated assault was the best they could hope for.

"We the jury find the defendant, Ernest W. Yeoman…" The foreman paused. "Guilty."

The courtroom was suddenly abuzz with whisperings, mumblings and a few shouts, gasps and cheers.

The judge banged his gavel and the din quieted as the foreman went on to read guilty verdicts for conspiracy to commit aggravated assault on two public officials and conspiracy to kidnap a public official.

It took Dani a split second to process everything the foreman had said. They'd done it. Yeoman was going to prison. Based on the verdicts, it sounded as though he'd be in prison for a very long time.

She felt light-headed. Then she realized that quite a bit of the noise in the courtroom was coming from the defendant's table.

Yeoman was up in his attorney's face. "What the hell?" he shouted. "You incompetent son of—"

The judge pounded his gavel. "Silence!" he snapped. "Silence. Guards!"

The guards were already on Yeoman. They grabbed him and cuffed him. All the while Yeoman continued to curse Drury.

Felix Drury, on the other hand, had abandoned his attempt to quiet his client. "Your Honor! Your Honor! May I approach the bench?" he shouted over his client's curses and the gallery's whispers and mumblings.

The judge was ignoring Yeoman. He looked at Drury over his glasses. "No, you may not." He banged the gavel again and shouted, "This court is adjourned." He thanked the jurors, then stood and left the courtroom.

Natalie Shallowford turned to Dani. She smiled and held her arms out.

Dani came around through the gate and hugged her. "Great job," she said. "Thank you so much."

"Oh, honey, Harte had all the paperwork in order. And your testimony, not only about the night of your grandfather's death, but your ordeal the night of the storm, cinched it."

"Oh," she said, gripping the bar that divided the courtroom from the visitors' gallery. She covered her mouth with her hand.

"Dani, are you okay?"

She nodded. "I am. For the first time since the night Granddad died, I'm okay." She blinked away the burning behind her eyelids. "He's really going to prison."

Natalie squeezed her shoulder. "I'm so glad. And don't forget, the three men who attacked your grandfather are going to prison too, on plea agreements."

Dani nodded. "Thank you again, Natalie."

Natalie waved a hand, then turned to pick up the piles of papers and cram them into her briefcase.

Dani turned toward Harte. Her knees felt weak and she had to grasp the back of a chair to steady herself. She hadn't seen him since the EMTs had put him in the ambulance at Paul Guillame's house. She'd been locked up in that damned hotel room while he'd lain in the hospital fighting for his life.

He looked so awful. Pale and thin and—almost breakable. And it was her fault. He'd protected her and doing so had nearly killed him.

He smiled the crooked smile that made her heart hurt. Somehow, she managed to walk up to him, even though her knees still felt boneless.

"What are you doing here?" she asked. "Your surgery was only four days ago." A movement to Harte's left caught her eye. It was Lucas, approaching. She turned an accusing gaze on him. "He shouldn't be here," she snapped.

"Yeah? Try telling him that," Lucas shot back. "I'll be outside." He put his hand on Harte's shoulder. "Try not to undo all the work the surgeon did, okay, kid?"

Harte gave him a brief nod. "I wanted to be here," he said. His voice sounded hollow. "So, Natalie did a great job. Congratulations. Yeoman's going to prison."

"She said you did all the work," she responded.

He shrugged, then winced. "So you can go home now. No more 'incarceration.'"

"Yeah. I'm not even sure I believe Yeoman's really going to prison yet. It's a lot to process." She gestured toward Harte's arm. "So how—how are you doing?" she asked, working to keep her tone light.

An odd expression flickered across his face. "I'm doing okay. Mom's taking care of me."

She noticed his hand was white-knuckled on the chair arm. "I'm glad," she said. "Let her spoil you."

"I don't have much of a choice right now."

She nodded, looking at his hand, wanting so badly to touch it. "Lucas told me that the surgery was touch-and-go—" Her voice gave out. She cleared her throat. "I mean—"

He inclined his head. "It was, although I didn't know it until it was all over. The first thing I remember after they put me in the ambulance is waking up in the hospital. Ethan was there, looking exhausted and worried."

"Everybody was worried about you."

The crooked smile played about his mouth again. But the smile didn't reach his eyes. "I know," he said. "A lot of people came by—and called."

Dani winced. "I wanted to call. I asked Lucas about you, but he said your family was there. And that's who you needed. You needed to rest and get better with your parents and your brothers around you." The more she said, the lamer her excuses sounded. But what was she supposed to say?

Get well soon? Thanks for keeping me alive and for taking a bullet for me? By the way, did the mind-blowing sex mean anything to you?

She'd been his star witness. He'd taken care of her, protected her, made sure the bad guys didn't kill her. He'd have been here in the prosecutor's chair, fighting for justice for her granddad, if he'd been able. But it was over now. He'd done what he had to do. He'd go back to being a prosecutor and a Delancey, and she'd go back to being a public defender.

"Dani, it's okay. I understand. We Delanceys can be intimidating."

She shook her head. "You almost died. You needed your family. Besides, I was in good hands with Natalie. She's a good prosecutor. Not as good as you, I didn't mean that. I mean, you're both good."

Harte grimaced at Dani's words and her tone.

She continued, talking too rapidly. "So the judge didn't talk about sentencing. When do you think it will be?" Her hands twisted in her lap.

He put his hand over hers to still them. "Dani, stop."

She looked up, a faint panic showing in her eyes. He had no idea if she was afraid he was going to say something intimate, or afraid he wasn't.

"Tell me what's the matter?" he asked warily.

Her hand squeezed his. She closed her eyes. "I—I'm not sure. I know Yeoman's going to prison. I know you're going to be okay. I should be happy to get back to my normal life."

She straightened and looked at him, uttering a short laugh. "I thought I was afraid of storms. But that was a childish phobia. When I saw you lying on the floor bleeding, when I thought we were going to be killed and I couldn't do anything—I realized that is real fear. Fear of how easily all this—" She waved a hand. "Our lives can be cut short. That's a fear I'm not sure will ever go away."

Harte's throat tightened. The pain of his wound didn't hurt nearly as much as seeing her like this. She had learned a horrible lesson, and it had destroyed her last childish belief—that fear was all about oneself, and there was always a stronger person who could wipe it away.

"I know," he said. "When I felt the bullet hit me, I was sure that was it. I was dead."

She made a strangled sound.

"But that didn't scare me nearly as much as the thought that I'd be leaving you alone." He closed his eyes. "I've never been that afraid before."

"You thought of me?" she said. Her tone was reverent.

"Of course I did. If I could, I'd make sure you never had to feel afraid again." He squeezed her hand.

"There's nothing I'd like better," she murmured.

"Do you mean that?" His voice was subdued. He pulled her hand toward him and pressed her fingers against his lips.

She swallowed, her gaze on his lips against her knuckles. Then she looked at him. "Except maybe to make sure you're always safe."

He smiled at her. To his surprise, her eyes immediately welled up with tears. She swiped at them as if they were flies.

"I swear to you I never cry," she said, sniffling.

"Yeah, right," he said as he leaned toward her, pulling on her hand. She sat forward and kissed him gently on the lips.

He wanted more, wanted to pull her to him and kiss her hard and long. He wanted to do more than kiss her, but every time he moved, his bound shoulder seized in pain, reminding him of how close that bullet had been to his heart.

Dani pulled her head back and looked at him. "So, what now?" she asked.

"What now?" He smiled at her. "I'd like to pick you up and carry you off to my bed. But I don't think that's going to happen for a while." He shifted in the chair and winced. "The best I can offer you right now is the opportunity to lie beside me and watch me sleep, occasionally fetch me a glass of water and help me get to my feet when I need to."

"That sounds wonderful, as long as you promise to slay dragons for me."

"That, my lady, is what I live for."

* * * * *

#1419 THE MARSHAL'S HOSTAGE
The Marshals of Maverick County
Delores Fossen
Marshal Dallas Walker is none too happy to learn his old flame, Joelle Tate, is reopening a cold case where he is one of her prime suspects.

#1420 SPECIAL FORCES FATHER
The Delancey Dynasty
Mallory Kane
A Special Forces operative and a gutsy psychiatrist must grapple with a ruthless kidnapper—and their unflagging mutual attraction—to save the child she never wanted him to know about.

#1421 THE PERFECT BRIDE
Sutton Hall Weddings
Kerry Connor
To uncover the truth about her friend's death, Jillian Jones goes undercover as a bride-to-be at a mysterious mansion, soon drawing the suspicions of the manor's darkly handsome owner—and the attention of a killer....

#1422 EXPLOSIVE ATTRACTION
Lena Diaz
A serial bomber fixates on Dr. Darby Steele and only police detective Rafe Morgan can help her. Together they try to figure out how she became the obsession of a madman before she becomes the next victim.

#1423 PROTECTING THEIR CHILD
Angi Morgan
Texas Ranger Cord McCrea must escape through the west Texas mountains with his pregnant ex-wife to stay one step ahead of the deadly gunman who has targeted his entire family.

#1424 BODYGUARD LOCKDOWN
Donna Young
Booker McKnight has sworn revenge on the man who killed fifty men—Booker's men. His bait? The only woman he's ever loved. The problem? She doesn't know.

You can find more information on upcoming Harlequin® titles, free excerpts and more at www.Harlequin.com.

REQUEST YOUR FREE BOOKS!
2 FREE NOVELS PLUS 2 FREE GIFTS!

H HARLEQUIN®

INTRIGUE®

BREATHTAKING ROMANTIC SUSPENSE

YES! Please send me 2 FREE Harlequin Intrigue® novels and my 2 FREE gifts (gifts are worth about $10). After receiving them, if I don't wish to receive any more books, I can return the shipping statement marked "cancel." If I don't cancel, I will receive 6 brand-new novels every month and be billed just $4.49 per book in the U.S. or $5.24 per book in Canada. That's a savings of at least 14% off the cover price! It's quite a bargain! Shipping and handling is just 50¢ per book in the U.S. and 75¢ per book in Canada.* I understand that accepting the 2 free books and gifts places me under no obligation to buy anything. I can always return a shipment and cancel at any time. Even if I never buy another book, the two free books and gifts are mine to keep forever.

182/382 HDN FVQV

Name _____ (PLEASE PRINT) _____

Address _____ Apt. #

City _____ State/Prov. _____ Zip/Postal Code

Signature (if under 18, a parent or guardian must sign)

Mail to the **Harlequin® Reader Service:**
IN U.S.A.: P.O. Box 1867, Buffalo, NY 14240-1867
IN CANADA: P.O. Box 609, Fort Erie, Ontario L2A 5X3
**Are you a subscriber to Harlequin Intrigue books
and want to receive the larger-print edition?
Call 1-800-873-8635 or visit www.ReaderService.com.**

* Terms and prices subject to change without notice. Prices do not include applicable taxes. Sales tax applicable in N.Y. Canadian residents will be charged applicable taxes. Offer not valid in Quebec. This offer is limited to one order per household. Not valid for current subscribers to Harlequin Intrigue books. All orders subject to credit approval. Credit or debit balances in a customer's account(s) may be offset by any other outstanding balance owed by or to the customer. Please allow 4 to 6 weeks for delivery. Offer available while quantities last.

Your Privacy—The Harlequin® Reader Service is committed to protecting your privacy. Our Privacy Policy is available online at www.ReaderService.com or upon request from the Harlequin Reader Service.

We make a portion of our mailing list available to reputable third parties that offer products we believe may interest you. If you prefer that we not exchange your name with third parties, or if you wish to clarify or modify your communication preferences, please visit us at www.ReaderService.com/consumerschoice or write to us at Harlequin Reader Service Preference Service, P.O. Box 9062, Buffalo, NY 14269. Include your complete name and address.

HI13

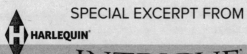
THE MARSHAL'S HOSTAGE
by USA TODAY bestselling author
Delores Fossen

*A sexy U.S. marshal and a feisty bride-to-be must go on
the run when danger from their past resurfaces....*

"Where the hell do you think you're going?" Dallas demanded.

But he didn't wait for an answer. He hurried to her, hauled her onto his shoulder caveman-style and carried her back into the dressing room.

That's when she saw the dark green Range Rover squeal to a stop in front of the church.

Owen.

Joelle struggled to get out of Dallas's grip, but he held on and turned to see what had captured her attention. Owen, dressed in a tux, stepped from the vehicle and walked toward his men. She had only seconds now to defuse this mess.

"I have to talk to him," she insisted.

"No. You don't," Dallas disagreed.

Joelle groaned because that was the pigheaded tone she'd encountered too many times to count.

"I'll be the one to talk to Owen," Dallas informed her. "I want to find out what's going on."

Joelle managed to slide out of his grip and put her feet on the floor. She latched on to his arm to stop him from going to the door. "You can't. You have no idea how bad things can get if you do that."

He stopped, stared at her. "Does all of this have something to do with your report to the governor?"

She blinked, but Joelle tried to let that be her only reaction. "No."

"Are you going to tell me what this is all about?" Dallas demanded.

"I can't. It's too dangerous." Joelle was ready to start begging him to leave. But she didn't have time to speak.

Dallas hooked his arm around her, lifted her and tossed her back over his shoulder.

"What are you doing?" Joelle tried to get away, tried to get back on her feet, but he held on tight.

Dallas threw open the dressing room door and started down the hall with her. "I'm kidnapping you."

Be sure to pick up
THE MARSHAL'S HOSTAGE
by USA TODAY *bestselling author Delores Fossen,*
on sale April 23 wherever
Harlequin Intrigue books are sold!